The Runaway Wife

Book 4 in The Brides of Little Creede Series

by
CiCi Cordelia

ISBN: 979-8-9918608-3-3

www.CiCiCordelia.com

ACKNOWLEDGEMENT:

To our Betas:

Over the course of writing the BRIDES OF LITTLE CREEDE Series, our beta readers have enthusiastically offered support, ideas, invaluable critique, and thus helped us immeasurably.

Thanks so much!

Chapter 1

Little Creede, Colorado
August, 1882

Sam Singleton mopped the back of his neck with an already-damp bandana. The breeze coming off the Lower Bountiful reduced the hot sun overhead from sweltering to uncomfortable, ruffling some of the picnic blankets spread out over schoolhouse grounds. The heated air rang with shouts, giggles, and feminine shrieks as children ran circles around their folks, ignoring admonishments and scolding fingers.

He caught the suspenders of a rowdy youngster barreling into him. "Slow down. Before you hurt somebody."

The freckled carrot-top stared up at Sam with rounded eyes bluer than the sky above. His slack jaw revealed three missing front teeth as he hung in Sam's grip. "I ain't done nothin'. Leggo, or I'll tell my paw."

Ornery little boys, the ones boasting all attitude and mouth, often irritated the hell out of him. "Who's your paw?" Sam growled. He leaned down until his nose was inches from the child's, whose smirk changed to panic.

He squirmed against Sam's hold, to no avail. "I ain't tellin' an' yew can't make me." A bead of sweat trickled down his grubby face. "Yew gonna run me outta town on a rail?"

His temper easing, Sam released a sharp snort. Hot days irritated him too, and this kid wasn't any brattier than half the boys in town. He set the rascal on his feet and straightened the crooked shirt and patched britches. "Go on now, find your folks. And stay out of trouble or I'll be having a talk with your paw."

The boy took off on a tear, speeding toward the shade of a sprawling juniper where a large family overflowed the edges of a faded quilt. At the last moment he turned and stuck out his tongue.

In response, Sam danced his fingers over his holstered Colt and bit back a grin at the way the kid's eyes bugged out, before he disappeared into the clot of children scattered over the quilt.

Tipping down the brim of his brown felted slouch to block the sun, Sam kept to the outskirts of the festivities. He'd already been offered plenty of food, accepting a chicken leg here and a plate of cookies there, his grunting version of gratitude met with uncertain smiles and a couple of matronly titters.

He'd rarely spoken more than a few dozen words to anyone outside of his place of business and several other locals he considered friends. Half the town probably thought he was a miserable bastard; he'd wager the rest understood his real occupation involved making certain nothing untoward happened when folks came to gamble.

These days, a lot of men patronized Gleason's Gambling Galleria regularly, and it was Sam's responsibility to his boss, Knight Gleason, to see winners and losers alike moving on amicably. It was a duty he viewed seriously since his arrival a year ago. If his overall demeanor sometimes took on a dour cast because of that duty, then so be it.

Sam gained the wooden boardwalk, striding past various businesses and shops, more than ready to put the crowds behind him and get back to the Galleria. He'd spotted Sheriff Joshua Lang along with a few of the local deputies, enjoying their family time. He had grudging respect for the way Lang and his staff patrolled Little Creede and the outlying areas of Rocky Gulch, as far north as Prairie Lick. The man's level of dedication was admirable even if it was the sort of work Sam wouldn't choose for himself.

As he approached the Galleria porch, shadowed against the bright afternoon sun, he offered a tip of the hat to Hannah Gleason, busy watering the flowering pots hanging along the sturdy awning. The woman was sweeter than candy and the perfect foil for her husband's blustering, bigger than life personality. "Missus Gleason, those posies of yours are looking mighty pretty." It was easy to swallow his usual gruffness and act politely toward his boss's wife.

She offered a happy smile amid rosy cheeks. "Thank you kindly, Mister Samuel." She fussed with the edges of a bright red flower. "The gardenias seem especially large this year."

Sam squinted at the fat petals of an unfamiliar flower. "That's what they're called?"

He would never tell her of the significance of hanging red flowers on a front porch. A genteel lady like Hannah didn't need to learn anything about the seedier side of life. Something Sam was all too aware of, having grown up in an orphanage from a young age before running off in search of a better life.

"Yes. For some reason, Knight kept trying to get me to plant those white begonias the Carter twins dug up in back of the Mercantile." Giving the heavy flowers a final caress, she bent to lift the watering bucket at her feet. "I do so love red."

Sam jumped to her side and scooped it up first.

She beamed at him, rubbing her belly. "I could have gotten it."

"Your man would skin me alive if I allowed you to lift things in your condition." His gaze dropped toward her roundness, visible beneath her increasing gown.

Sam hurried ahead to open the front doors of the Galleria, allowing Hannah to enter first. "I'll take your bucket to the kitchen. You go and put up your feet."

She turned to regard him appraisingly. "A woman in the family way doesn't faze you at all, does it, Mister Singleton?"

"Nope. Do I need to beg your pardon for such an unseemly attitude?"

"Not in the least." With a wink, the First Lady of Gleason's Galleria made for the second floor, where her husband kept an expansive office.

Sam headed to the kitchen, shaking his head ruefully. Something about the delicate Hannah always brought out the gentleman—albeit rusty and unused—in him.

The kitchen was deserted this time of day, not surprising since most of the staff were still enjoying themselves at the picnic. Sam set the can on the floor near the wide farmer sink Knight had installed six months ago. Dolores Lund, the Galleria's cook, kept the kitchen spotless and had vowed eternal devotion to Gleason after he'd presented her with the new sink and counterspace. Sam'd never seen a woman carry on so, over kitchen things, no less.

At the end of the counter sat a fancy glass plate cradling a luscious two-crust pie. He sniffed the air appreciatively. By the rich fragrance, Sam guessed cherry, recently pulled from the oven. His mouth watered despite his already stuffed stomach. Maybe Dolores wouldn't mind if he snuck a thin wedge—

Searching for the pie server, a thump and a muffled oath brought him up short. He spun toward the sound, coming from the cavernous pantry where most of the dry goods and supplies were stored.

Silently he advanced across the large room, drawing his gun as a precaution. He wouldn't put it past some drunken sot to stagger in from one of the gaming rooms, searching for money, thinking any Galleria staff would be dumb enough to keep a safe in here.

The pantry door stood open an inch. The whisper of rustling and more muttering hovered in the air. Tensing, he readied for possible danger. Thumbing the latch, he brought up his gun arm and yanked hard.

A mound of tattered clothes and dark curls tumbled out of the opening, landing on the floor at his feet. *What the—*?

Sam bent and caught a thin, flailing arm, jerking the thief upright. From the cracked, scuffed boots to the downcast head of tangled, choppy hair, this was no gambler desperate for extra coins, only a young boy starving for something to eat. Narrow-shouldered, dressed in torn trousers and a shirt studded with burdock stickers, the kid could probably cram an entire cherry pie into his gullet and his britches would still slide down his backside.

Tamping down any feelings of sympathy, he marched the now-struggling pantry poacher across the kitchen and shoved him into the nearest chair. The boy tried to bolt, so Sam gripped one bony shoulder. "Stay put and tell me who you are."

A dirt-encrusted face raised to his. "Let me go!"

He frowned, taking a more focused look at the boy. Full lips. High cheekbones underneath the crud. Long lashes framed remarkable blue-gray eyes. Delicate ears were visible from between the shorn locks.

"You're a girl." She squirmed in her seat and made to escape. Sam's grip tightened, holding her in place. "You're not going anywhere, missy." He hooked another chair on the toe of his boot and dragged it over to block her in, trapping her against the wall until she had no choice except to remain still. "Start talking."

Her grimy fist pounded the table surface. "You've no right to keep me here."

Sam didn't have time for this foolishness. "Your name. *Now.*"

She strained against his hold on her shoulder and spat out, "Izzy." Her mouth firmed. "Now, let go."

"Last name." He gave her a brief shake. "I'm fast losing patience, and our jail doesn't have any niceties for females."

At the mention of jail, what color remained in those high cheekbones leeched out. "Don't lock me up! I only wanted a place to rest and maybe something to eat." Dejection came off her in waves. "My name is Izzy McDougall. Please don't stick me behind bars."

He eased up on his grip, cupping her shoulder with more care to examine her, looking for lies and finding nothing more than a scared girl. If she was more than eighteen or nineteen, he'd eat his hat for supper.

Judging by what he now determined were bruises underneath all that dirt and grime, he realized someone had mistreated her. Anger tightened his jaw. Where her ragged shirt gapped, a man's fingerprints marred her slender neck. Doubtful a woman would have such a large grip.

A growl rumbled in his throat. The urge to track down whoever'd hurt her—and beat the snot out of them—rose swiftly inside him.

Her eyes widened, and she shrank away.

Sam immediately released her and eased back into his chair, so he wasn't towering over her. "I won't hurt you."

She didn't reply, only continued to watch him with suspicion. The uneven ends of her hair indicated she'd chopped it off with a blunt blade.

Disguising herself as a boy.

Her feet were covered in a pair of the rattiest boots he'd ever seen. Mud spattered, they appeared to be at least two sizes too big with a hole in the left toe. He flicked a glance back to her and held steady. "How long have you been on the road?"

She hesitated, mumbling, "Not sure. A week, maybe more."

Good Christ.

"You've had nothing to eat since?"

One birdlike shoulder raised in a shrug. "I stole some eggs from a chicken coop." At his frown she added, "About three days ago."

No wonder she'd raided the place for food. Raw eggs and then nothing for three days. With a grunt, Sam got to his feet. When it looked like she might try to flee, he cast her a warning glance. "Sit tight, girl. I'll get you something to eat. You can stay here for now. Staff quarters are safe and nobody'll bother you."

He turned toward the largest icebox, another newfangled item Knight had ordered, to the delight of Dolores. Usually packed full of her excellent cooking, today he found a plate of roast chicken and a bowl of bread pudding.

Returning to the table, he ignored Izzy's eye-popping gape at the amount of food and pushed the chicken toward her. "Go on, eat."

She lifted a trembling hand, but quickly dropped it back onto the table. "I'm dirty."

"Pretty much." Stepping to the sink, Sam pumped enough water to fill the dish basin Dolores kept on the counter and dipped a dishrag in to wet it. He brought it to her. "Wash up. I'll get you some milk."

As he rooted in a cupboard for a tumbler, from the corner of his eye he saw her wipe off before grabbing for a drumstick, cramming in the food as if he'd take it from her any second.

Having gone hungry more than once during his childhood—not to mention being on the receiving end of a few mean beatings during his years at the orphanage—Sam understood what she must have dealt with already.

He bought the tall tumbler of milk over to the table, setting it down along with a dry dish towel in lieu of a napkin. Taking a seat, he watched as she gobbled down the chicken. Removing the dirty plate, he placed a saucer of bread pudding in front of her. He sat by silently while she dug in, pausing between swallows to gulp the milk.

"What's your name?" she mumbled around a mouthful of pudding.

"Samuel Singleton." He inclined his head briefly. "I never heard of anyone called Izzy. Got a full name?"

"My real name is Isadora. But I prefer answering to Izzy." Her gaze dropped to the mess of chicken bones, empty tumbler, and pudding crumbs she'd left on the table. "I—thank you for the food. I can clean it all up." Her eyes met his, for the first time shining with something other than defiance. "I can do a lot of household things. Polishing, mopping. I can cook, too."

Even he wasn't big enough of a rotter to throw her into the streets, obviously on the run from someone. He had no doubt Dolores would take the girl under her wing.

"Missus Lund is the boss of the kitchen at the Galleria and does all the hiring. What she says goes, but I'm sure she could use some extra help." At Izzy's eager nod, Sam held up a cautionary hand. "I'm in charge of security, and I'll need to know where you're from, how old you are, and what sort of trouble you're in."

"I'm not—"

"Don't finish that lie." He couldn't do his job if he didn't know what he was facing. "If you're bringing danger to the Galleria, you'd best tell me now."

Izzy glanced away. She picked up the towel and used it to wipe her mouth with awkward thoroughness. Long moments passed while he waited her out.

Finally, she folded the cloth neatly and laid it on the table before she met his gaze. "I'm nineteen, old enough to take care of myself. Please don't ask me anything more."

"Do I need to worry about someone coming to Little Creede to find you?"

Sadness shone in her eyes, then she squared her shoulders. "No one cares where I am, Mister Singleton."

"Just Sam." He pushed back his chair. "C'mon. Let's see what Missus Lund has to say."

Chapter 2

Plopping down on the comfortable bed, Izzy studied the room Dolores Lund had provided for her. She had to pinch herself, unable to believe her good fortune. The mid-sized room contained furnishings of good quality, from the bright quilt covering the feather-tick mattress, to the table and chairs in one corner that matched the carved oak washstand with its decorative painted bowl and pitcher. A fireplace on an opposite wall, already set with kindling and split logs, delighted her. Images of sitting in front of a toasty fire in the dead of winter filled her mind.

If I'm even still here. She tried not to fall into melancholy.

The heady fragrance of flowers hung in the air. Finding a generous cake of soap along with a soft linen towel, Izzy had happily availed herself of a decent sponge bath.

She appreciated the starched white uniform and apron Missus Lund had lent her. Though loose and too long, the dress felt smooth against her skin. Gratitude swamped her. This morning she'd been dirty, tired, and hungry, with the prospect of another night sleeping in whatever cramped space she could find offering her shelter. Now, she'd been fed and allowed some time to rest and perform much-needed ablutions.

Even her new position, helping Missus Lund in the kitchen, brought on gratefulness. After scrubbing the luncheon dishes, her skin was red and chapped from the harsh lye soap and hot water, yet the satisfaction of a job well done was worth any discomfort. She'd been offered a dab of rosewater salve to rub into the worst of the damage.

Until recently, she'd never been required to do menial tasks. Her father's business had provided their family with an affluent lifestyle, including a cook and two maids to run the house and a gardener assigned to the outer grounds. Izzy would have traded it all for a modicum of kindness from him.

William McDougall only cared about her brother Willy.

Two years ago, her mother disappeared. One by one the staff left—either voluntarily or by dismissal, Izzy never discovered—until she found herself alone in a house with menfolk who appeared to hate her. Required to take the place of several live-in workers, she'd toiled long, tiring hours in a house too big for only three people to occupy. Nothing she did seemed to please Father or Willy, and both let her know regularly of her many failings.

Verbal abuse eventually turned physical, and more than once she went to bed with marks on her back and legs from the punishment Father seemed to enjoy doling out. If she protested or talked back, the additional torture of being locked in her room joined the beatings. Izzy prayed for enough fortitude to survive the desolation of what her life had become, thinking sooner or later he'd find something else to amuse himself . . .

Until one night she'd overheard them discussing her mother. Horror had flooded Izzy when the tone of their conversation turned dark, dangerous . . . threatening. Had they plotted to kill Mother? Had they succeeded?

A knock at the door pulled Izzy from further morose thoughts, and she jumped to her feet. She'd been told the chores were done for the rest of the afternoon, and she wasn't expected back in the kitchen unless any of the Galleria patrons chose to indulge in dinner, usually served family-style.

"Y-Yes," she called out, fearful her father had managed to track her down.

"Hello, Izzy. It's Hannah Gleason. Knight's wife. May I come in?"

Not wanting to keep her employer's wife waiting, she quickly crossed the room. Why would this woman seek her out? Izzy wasn't anyone important. *Is she going to dismiss me?* Dolores had appeared happy with the thoroughness of her work. She thought back to her time in the kitchen, trying to determine if she'd done something wrong.

Drawing in a deep breath, Izzy swung open the door. A petite, brunette woman with exquisite pale brown eyes peered out from a stack of gowns she held in her arms.

"Hello, sweet girl." Missus Gleason crossed the room to arrange the gowns on the bed. She turned back with a welcoming smile. Izzy noticed her belly, swollen with child beneath a simple yet elegant linen gown. "Samuel told me we had a new worker who would need some womanly things."

At a loss for words, tension tightened Izzy's stomach. It'd been so long since anyone had shown her any compassion or generosity, she didn't know how to react. Wasn't sure she could trust it.

Another voice trilled from the hallway. "I have more."

A young dark-haired woman paused at the open door. "I'm Vivian Lang. It's so very nice to meet you." Not waiting for an invite, she bustled in and dumped an assortment of what appeared to be petticoats and intimates on the bed. "Should we call you Isadora or Izzy?"

"Um. Izzy's fine." She nervously cleared her throat, unsure what to say. She wasn't accustomed to social niceties from unfamiliar women. Regarding both open, friendly faces, Izzy finally turned to her new employer. "Missus Gleason—"

She patted Izzy's cheek. "Please, call me Hannah."

The tender gesture was so like her mother's, it brought a rush of tears to her eyes. She quickly lowered her lashes. Biting her bottom lip until it stung, Izzy forced away her sadness. She'd already cried enough. If her father's cruelty had taught her anything, it was to never show weakness.

She stiffened her spine and looked directly at Hannah. "This is very generous of you, but I can't accept all these things. It's enough you offered me a position."

"Horsefeathers." She waved dismissively. "You're in Little Creede now, and we take care of our own."

Izzy opened her mouth to refuse again, until Vivian's musical laugh captured her attention. "I wouldn't bother arguing." She came over to stand next to them. "Don't let that sweet demeanor fool you, she's even more stubborn than her husband."

"*Harrumph.*" Hannah's lips twitched. "Knight is not stubborn."

Vivian snorted. "If you say so," she teased, rolling her eyes.

Izzy found herself fighting a smile, amused by their interaction. Under different circumstances, they might have become her friends. Now she didn't dare to form any attachments in case Father or Willy came looking for her.

I can't stay in one place too long.

"I'll introduce you to Knight at dinner," Hannah said. "Seven o'clock in the main hall."

Izzy shook her head. Beyond what Samuel Singleton had given her, Missus Lund had provided her with supper, and she didn't have money to pay for another. "I'm not hungry. After I finish my kitchen duties, I plan to get a good night's sleep, so I can work during breakfast."

As if calling her a liar, her stomach took the opportunity to loudly complain about another missed meal. Vivian arched two perfect eyebrows, while Hannah studied her skeptically.

"Maybe Samuel didn't explain. You get three meals a day with the position." Hannah rubbed her own rounded middle. "Goodness knows I'm always hungry these days and running Gleason's Gambling Galleria takes a lot of work. We'll need you at your best." She tried to intimidate with a stern look, but her face was too kind to be threatening. "Whether or not you return to the kitchen, I'll expect to see you at seven."

Vivian's eyes twinkled with mirth. "No use arguing, Izzy. As I said, stubborn."

Hannah chuckled. "Oh, hush." She gestured toward the bed, laden with apparel. "Since we've hours yet, why don't you pick out what fits? And do not argue. Madame Vivian here has already mentioned there's no use."

Izzy approached the colorful mound, nervously twisting jagged strands of her cropped hair. She loved beautiful clothes as much as the next young lady, except right now she couldn't seem to muster a single feminine instinct. It'd broken her heart to cut off what she had considered her very best feature.

Vivian touched Izzy's shoulder. "Would you like me to trim you a bit? I regularly even up my husband's hair—"

"Yes, though he balks with every inch you take away from him," Hannah put in, mischief in her tone. At Izzy's confused frown, Hannah explained, "Our dedicated and brave Sheriff Lang has the most glorious head of hair. Ladies simply melt, I tell you."

"Sheriff?" Izzy gulped, spinning toward the lovely Vivian. "You are married to a lawman?" She could feel her breath speeding up in her lungs and fought to keep her panic under control. Father or Willy—or both, heaven help her—could easily track her here if they started working with the law. What if they demanded her return? As a single young woman, she had no rights, couldn't stop them from taking her.

"Joshua is a most honorable and just sheriff." Vivian caught one of Izzy's hands. "My, what cold fingers. Tell you what. Pick out something to wear at least for tonight's dinner, and I'll come over early to help you ready yourself. I'll also trim your hair. I do believe you'll find a few ribbons in this lot. I can do wonders with a touch of pomade, too." She gently squeezed her hand. "It will be fun."

Izzy studied Vivian, searching for any sign of guile and finding only warm concern. A quick glance around the compact room proved she had indeed landed in a safe place. Perhaps she could relax somewhat, let down her guard, and release some of the tension keeping her poor muscles cramped and tight.

"All right, thank you." She pointed to a pile of sunny yellow, dotted with tiny blue flowers. "I like that one."

"Perfect," Hannah said approvingly. "How about a cup of afternoon tea? Dolores made molasses cookies yesterday. I'll go fetch a tray." She strode out, moving fast for a lady in her condition.

"I'll help," Vivian declared, following. At the threshold she turned with a wink and a smile. "One tea party coming up, Miss Izzy."

For a long moment Izzy stared after them, trying to remember the last time a stranger had treated her with such kindness. Emotion clogged her throat.

A long time, that's for sure.

Maybe she'd found a home in Little Creede with decent folks, after all.

Knight Gleason finished lighting his cigar and leaned back in his massive leather chair. "How's the lil' gal workin' out?"

Sam sank into the smaller, yet no less opulent chair across from his employer's desk, stretching his legs. "Haven't seen her since I handed her off to Dolores." He whipped a bandana out of his trouser pocket and blotted his forehead, thinking about how petite Izzy McDougall had appeared next to the robust Dolores Lund, who'd taken over as soon as Sam had led the bedraggled girl to the back quarters where some of the Galleria staff lived. With a sympathetic, "You poor thing," Dolores had produced a uniform for Izzy that would no doubt swim on her. Assuring her she'd have plenty of time to clean up and return to the kitchen for the luncheon chores, she hustled Izzy off to one of the empty rooms.

He met Knight's amused blue eyes. "You say something?"

"Ah might've asked yew if'n this Izzy is a purty lil' thing." He released a snort. "Ah kin see by the look in yer eyes, that she is. Yew find out what spooked her?"

"Some of it." Ignoring Knight's keen observation, Sam relayed what he knew.

A grimace crossed Knight's broad, weathered features at the mention of her bruises. He puffed on his cigar. "Poor child. Ah'm right glad yew found her." He stubbed out the remains of his cigar in the heavy wood and brass ash receptacle that matched the humidor cabinet at one end of his desk.

Sam raised his brows knowingly as Knight blew out the last mouthful of smoke.

"Don'tcha go tattlin' to the missus, now. Mah sweet Hannah thinks ah already stopped smokin' fer the babe. Ah figure ah got a month or two more to enjoy mahself." He released a booming laugh.

Sam's lips twitched. "I'll never tell." Getting to his feet, he slapped his slouch against his leg before dropping it back on his head. "I'm off to my afternoon checks. If I hear anything more on Miss McDougall, I'll let you know."

Exiting Knight's den, he strode toward the front receiving parlor, coming up short at the sight of a curly-haired female standing near the set of wide double windows overlooking the Galleria's settin' porch.

Wearing a kitchen uniform that hung on her slender frame, Izzy McDougall clutched the windowsill hard enough to whiten her knuckles. She stared outside, her breathing labored.

"Izzy?" When she didn't answer, Sam came abreast of her and looked outside to see what had upset her. A few townsfolk strolled along the main boardwalk. Nothing seemed unusual or out of place. "Izzy, what is it?" He touched her arm.

She whirled with a cry, shrinking back against the Priscilla curtains Hannah had proudly ordered from Natchez and he'd helped hang two months ago.

Lord, what now? "Something scare you?"

"Mi-Mister Singleton?" she stammered as he led her away from the window. Her entire disposition seemed odd, her expression pinched.

"Just Sam, honey." He took her elbow and guided her to one of the brocaded sofas scattered around the parlor, making sure her back was to the window. She sank down, forgetting to smooth her skirt beneath her legs, and he carefully took a seat next to her so he wouldn't stomp on the white cotton. He waited until she inhaled deeply, releasing a slow breath.

"Feeling better?"

"I'm all right." She couldn't quite meet his eyes. Sam resisted lifting her chin to better look her over. "It's only a cramp."

He cocked his head to examine her more closely. *Cramp, my ass.*

Unwilling to challenge her for fear of making things worse, he patted her hand instead. "You want a glass of water?" He'd rather see her down a shot of bourbon. Doubtful liquor had ever touched those innocent-looking lips, though.

"No. I'm fine, truly." She stood, forcing him to release her.

Before he could detain her further, she lifted her trailing skirt and raced across the parlor.

At the chime of the regulator near the side counter, Sam straightened his hat and smoothed down his vest, checking his holster fastenings.

Worry over the newest, most skittish townie would have to wait. He had duties that needed attending to.

Chapter 3

Izzy stared into the vanity mirror, running her palms over the yellow gown she wore, its nainsook weave, with its tiny blue flowers, particularly fine. In this heat the dress floated softly atop her petticoats and helped keep her cool. The below-elbow sleeves could be left down or pushed up, and the bodice and hemline seemed a perfect fit, too. Izzy could easily see either Vivian or Hannah wearing it, since both, like her, were small and slender.

She feathered two fingers across her exposed neck where a few light bruises remained. Not wanting to dwell on them, or how she'd gotten them, she eyed her hair instead. The trimmed-up tendrils rippled softly from the breeze coming in from her open window. A pretty blue ribbon held her chin-length curls out of her eyes. Vivian had indeed worked wonders with her rosewater pomade.

Yet Izzy's heart still lurched at the loss of her heavy, deep-brown locks. Her mother had loved fussing with the waist length mass, carefully brushing and braiding it every night. Having to cut it had been like losing the last connection with her.

I can always grow it back.

Pivoting away from the mirror, she crossed the room on bare feet. After escaping, her thin bedroom slippers had shredded from walking so many miles. A pair of shabby boots, left in a heap of rubbish near the last mining area she'd passed, had been all she could find to protect herself from rocks and stickers. The boots had been too big on her and blistered her heels. She couldn't bear the thought of wearing them again and doubted anyone would notice. She'd buy a pair of sensible shoes with her first wages.

As Izzy passed by the window, she suppressed a shiver, recalling the fellow she had seen striding down the section of street visible from the Galleria. From the cut of his coat to the dark hair peeking out from the stylish felt jaxon he wore at an angle, his familiar-looking appearance had made her clutch her chest in fear. She'd been afraid her father or brother had found her. A second, harder stare had assured her he was neither sire nor sibling.

She'd have to concoct some sort of explanation to Samuel for her obvious distress. Izzy doubted he would forget her frightened reaction at the window. He'd want to know why.

Maybe I need to tell him everything. The thought of discussing her family, and the abuse she'd endured, filled her with shame. What good would it do? Izzy didn't really believe Father or Willy cared enough to come looking for her.

A knock at her door got her pulse jittering. She expelled a shaky breath, swinging open the door. The object of her thoughts stood there.

"Hello," she said hesitantly. *Why is he here*? Did he intend to make her leave after all?

Samuel's gaze dropped down the length of her, then slowly rose back up.

She licked her lips, nervous tension coiling inside her.

His features relaxed. "You clean up nicely, Izzy."

"My hair's too short." She winced. *What a stupid thing to say.*

"Naw." At his amused drawl, she looked up in surprise. He smoothed a curl behind her ear. "It makes your eyes stand out." His finger traced the edge of her collar so lightly, she might have imagined it. "The flowers match their color."

"Oh." She had no idea how to respond to his statement.

For the past year, she'd been more house staff than daughter, and unless her father wanted to impress his business partners with glimpses of his 'devoted' children, Izzy had been kept isolated. Even before Mother's disappearance, opportunities to talk with anyone outside of her family had been rare. Never had she been in a man's presence by herself, until Samuel had dragged her out of the pantry.

He continued to hold her gaze, tilting his head, while she alternated between wanting to hide within her room, and trying not to gawk at how handsome he was. Wearing form-fitting trousers and a black vest stitched in burgundy, he cut a dashing figure. The hallway lamplight set off the gold in his dark-blond hair, turning his eyes a deeper brown. The hand he'd raised boasted a deep red garnet set in a signet ring he wore on his little finger.

When she thought she might not stand another moment of silence, he offered his arm. "Would you allow me to escort you to dinner, Miss Izzy?"

"How do you know I'm not going to the kitchen to work?" *Another stupid thing to say.* She barely resisted yanking her hair in frustration.

One eyebrow rose. "Because you're wearing such a pretty gown." He jiggled his arm as if to tempt her. "Dinner awaits, Izzy."

Telling herself he wouldn't let her refuse, Izzy placed her palm on his sleeve, the combination of soft cambric over hard muscle making her pulse jolt. As he led her to the dining salon, she concentrated on not stepping on the hem of her dress.

All during dinner, Sam observed, which was his job, his responsibility. He tracked the number of guests lounging at the dining tables, enjoying Dolores's excellent poached pork and pan biscuits, taking note of how many drank coffee or water; how many took to hard liquor. Those heavier drinkers would vacate their seats as soon as they gobbled down the last bite of blueberry buckle. After an appropriate amount of time he'd follow, maintaining his vigilance, one hand on his holster and the other tapping along to whatever tune the Galleria's resident piano player, Thaddeus Thorne, chose to plink out as the evening's entertainment.

Some of the gamblers would win, some would lose, and others might be drunkenly stupid enough to take their poor sportsmanship out on each other.

Different night, same game. Except tonight, the added fascination of Izzy McDougall, sitting primly across from him in her yellow gown—and bare feet—proved to be a distraction.

Sam swallowed a grin, thinking about those pink toes hidden under her skirts. He'd spotted them as he pulled out her chair and got her seated. Figuring she hoped no one noticed the lack of proper footwear, he'd kept quiet. He'd seen a dainty pair of slippers in the Mercantile's front window the other day and was confident they'd fit Izzy.

Tomorrow, I'll stop by and purchase them for her. If she balked, he'd tell her it'd come out of her first wages for her work at the Galleria.

Not that it would.

She appeared to enjoy being included within the Gleasons' circle. Knight was in his usual, larger-than-life element, and beside him, Hannah glowed like a pearl.

Knight's boisterous voice echoed around the room louder than buckshot. "Ah found yer silver dollar, darlin'," he boasted to his wife. "Nothin' up mah sleeve." He shook a bulging arm, then one big paw shot out to pluck something shiny from behind her ear. He offered it to her, and she giggled, clapping.

Having seen this trick more than a few times, Sam kept his attention on Izzy as Knight flashed a coin, rolling it between surprisingly nimble fingers. With laughing eyes, Izzy applauded along with Hannah each time the coin disappeared from Knight's knuckles, only to magically pop up under a butter dish or plate.

"How did you *do* that?" Izzy exclaimed. "I watched you so carefully."

"It's all in the wrist, Miss Isadora." Gleason shot her a wink.

She blushed. "You can call me Izzy."

"That's right kindly of yew," he replied gallantly. Holding up yet another coin, this one a half-cent, he deftly flipped over three china cups and snuck the cent-piece under the middle cup. "The hand is quicker than the eye, mah friends."

Sam settled back in his seat, one eye on the room and the other on his employer's antics, as both ladies gasped or cheered each time they chose the wrong cup to peek under.

Charmed by Knight Gleason and his enthusiastic determination to see to every comfort, Izzy couldn't recall enjoying an evening more. The gentlemanly way he treated his wife, and asked after each member of his staff, also revealed a lot about the strength of his character.

When he began his sleight of hand, pure delight and awe had her feeling happier and more entertained than she could ever recall.

She found herself laughing along with everyone else at the burly gambler's amusing stories of life on a Mississippi riverboat. "This heah rascal snuck aboard mah vessel durin' a storm." He pointed a blunt finger at Samuel. "Soppin' wet an' shiverin'. Asked fer bourbon, an' him barely old enough to grow peach fuzz under his lip, much less know what men drink." He raised his glass in a toast.

"If'n ah'd put whiskey in his scrawny gizzards, he'd a' fallen overboard."

Izzy tried to picture a younger version of Samuel, freezing cold and demanding hard liquor. Meeting his dark gaze across the table, she felt herself flush. Breaking eye contact, she asked, "Then what happened, Mister Gleason?"

"Why, ah kept him under mah tender wing. Fer a half-dozen yeahs or so, ah taught him everythin' ah know." Her host winked. "Ah'm right fortunate fer his expertise."

Throughout Mister Gleason's monologue, Samuel remained silent, his faint smile causing a fluttering sensation inside her that she couldn't decide was good or bad.

After dinner, he came around and pulled her chair back, offering her his arm. "I thought we could chat."

Izzy hesitated, confused. "Aren't I supposed to report to the kitchen?"

"Not on your first night here. Dolores told me you worked hard this afternoon. Anyway, Patsy from over at the Stage House came over a day early. She'll be serving in the dining salon for the next week or so. We can use the extra help for the tourney."

"Tourney?" she mumbled, as she allowed Samuel to pull her to her feet.

He led her down an unfamiliar hallway and into a side salon she'd only seen in passing. "The Galleria has a twice-yearly poker tourney. The next one begins in three days. The Miner Stage House is a restaurant and inn right down the street, owned by some friends of mine. Of the Gleasons, too. We'll stop by sometime and I'll introduce you. Patsy is a worker there and often helps out during tourneys."

He settled her onto a scarlet brocade chaise. Sitting next to her, he studied her with observant eyes. "Tell me why you were so afraid earlier today."

Resurgent fear clogged Izzy's throat, and for a long moment she couldn't speak.

Samuel took her hand and waited.

Feeling defensive, she blurted, "I said it was nothing. I had the hiccups and you startled me." When she tried to rise, he held her firmly in place. Inhaling a deep breath, holding it for a scant second, she slowly released it to retain her temper. "Mister Singleton, this isn't any of your concern."

"Just Sam, Izzy," he said in a patient tone.

"Missus Gleason calls you Samuel." She tugged against his grip again and shifted uncomfortably. "You're my employer, it doesn't feel right to be so forward."

"No, Mister Gleason is your employer. Mine as well. Besides, you and I are friends now, and if something scared you to the point you jumped about a foot off the floor and turned white as a ghost . . ." He trailed off, stroking the back of her hand in a motion probably meant to soothe. "I'm responsible for the security and safety of the Galleria. I extend my protection to the townsfolk because we take care of each other around here. If trouble's coming to Little Creede, I need to know."

Izzy regarded him closely, searching for any speck of deceit or false earnestness, and found only concern. "For a moment I thought I saw someone from my family. I realize now I was mistaken."

She tugged free of his grip. "I really need to go, Mister Singleton. I thought I'd spend a bit of time with Hannah this evening."

"Somehow I think I'm being fobbed off with an excuse." He stood and stretched out an elbow to help her up. "C'mon, I'll escort you to Missus Hannah's sitting room."

"Oh, you don't have to do that." Izzy avoided his proffered arm. She hadn't actually made plans with Hannah, and for all she knew the poor woman was exhausted and already in bed.

Samuel wouldn't be deterred. He grasped her shoulders and carefully lifted her to her feet. "I'll see you upstairs. After all, you could become lost."

Unable to figure a way to forestall him and finding herself half irritated, half touched at his persistence, Izzy capitulated, allowing him to guide her out of the salon toward the staircase leading up to Hannah's sitting room.

The old man paced the length of his study. Each thump of his shoes sent a twinge of pain through Willy's head. Sitting on the hard-as-a-rock settee Father had bought because it was fancy rather than comfortable, he waited, resisting the urge to rub at his aching temple where his sister's unwarranted attack days ago had done the most damage.

Stupid bitch.

Planting himself in front of the window, Father pulled back the heavy drapes to look at the dark street below. Silence stretched out for long moments, tightening the tension already present.

Leaning his head back against the settee cushion, Willy muttered, "Let's get this over with so I can go to bed."

The old man turned from the window and stomped his way across the room, looming over him. The cigar and bourbon stench of his breath made Willy's stomach churn sickeningly. "You're worthless and an idiot. Is that what you want to hear? You let a skinny little girl get the better of you." He bent down to glare at Willy. "You should have been on her tail a week ago. Why haven't you gone after her yet?"

"I was bleeding like a stuck pig, wasn't I? Couldn't even get out of bed until this morning," Willy protested. He struggled to sit up, rubbing his throbbing forehead.

"Because you're a weak milquetoast like your mother." Father grabbed him by the arm and shook until Willy's teeth rattled and his brain felt like exploding. "Get on your horse and find your sister. She's got duties to honor."

He let go, flinging Willy against the settee. "Dammit, old man—"

"Oh, toughen up, for God's sake. You want to succeed in the family business? Here's your first task. Find your sister and bring her home to see to her duties." Father strode to the door, slamming it shut behind him.

"Bastard," Willy mumbled, staggering to the sideboard to uncork the brandy. Fumbling for a clean glass, he poured himself a healthy dram and downed the potent drink in a few gulps. He relished the burn, before slamming the empty tumbler on the smeared surface.

The entire room smelled of stale dust, further proof of Isadora's perfidious treachery. The house had fast fallen into disrepair.

Shuffling to the door, Willy wiped a shirtsleeve across his mouth, uncaring of his father's order to head out tonight. He'd go when he was ready, and not before.

I'll bring her back, all right—he rubbed his still sore head—*after I make her pay for disrespecting me.*

Chapter 4

On his way to the Mercantile for one of Betsy Loman's buttermilk pies, Sam noticed a fancy-dressed stranger dismounting his horse in front of the jailhouse. He squinted against the bright sun, studying the dapper figure.

Do I know him?

Abandoning the pie, Sam changed course and made for the jailhouse. As he drew nearer, the man's gaze caught his for a moment before he turned away and entered the front office.

He'd bet money the dandy was related to Izzy. They had the same curly dark hair and facial features. Did he also have unusual blue-gray eyes like the scared and battered girl Sam had discovered in the pantry only a few days ago? He appeared to be near her age, perhaps a few years older, and could be a brother or a cousin.

Anger tightened Sam's spine at the thought the man might be the one responsible for the abuse he'd seen on her. She'd refused to say much the other night, although she'd revealed enough for him to understand her need to avoid family members. If Izzy had any relatives she could trust, she surely would have told him.

Then again, why would she trust him? She barely knew him.

Something I intend to remedy soon.

Inside, he found Joshua Lang holding a tintype photograph.

"—I'm her brother, and we're very concerned about her. Have you seen her, Sheriff?"

Joshua glanced up when he entered, and Sam gave his head a subtle shake. Neither he nor the local law should share any information on Izzy until they determined this stranger wasn't a threat. He could be lying about being her brother.

Lang raised a curious brow, passing the tintype back. "Sorry, haven't seen her."

"Howdy, Sheriff." Sam crossed the cluttered office, pausing next to the two men. "Got a moment? I'd like to discuss security for the upcoming poker tourney." He met the stranger's stare, eyes a direct match to the frightened woman he'd found in the pantry. "Haven't seen you around these parts. Here for the games?"

The stranger seemed friendly enough, yet the hard gleam in his regard indicated otherwise. "Name's Willy McDougall." He thrust his hand out and Sam had no choice but to reciprocate. "I'm looking for my sister, Isadora." He flipped the tintype over so Sam could see it.

Sam stared at the somewhat blurry image, recognizing Izzy. She wore an elegant gown and sat on a tufted sofa in a stately room filled with assorted riches. Obviously, she came from wealth. What struck him instantly was the deep sadness in her expressive gaze.

His distrust grew. "I haven't seen her."

McDougall muttered under his breath and shoved the tintype back into his pocket. "If you do, we have a thousand-dollar reward for her safe return."

"We'll be sure and let you know," Joshua said. "Where can we contact you?"

McDougall produced a slip of paper. "Send us a telegram, and we'll come fetch her."

"If we see her."

"Appreciate it." McDougall exited abruptly.

Sam stepped to the door and made sure he headed out of town.

Joshua joined him. "What's that all about, Singleton?"

"Found his sister laying low at the Galleria a few days ago." Sam pointed to the paper the sheriff held. "Let's have a look."

Joshua unfolded the paper and glanced at it. "Silver Cache. Must be where the family lives." He eyeballed Sam. "Wanna tell me why we didn't inform her brother?"

"She's running from something, Lang. Caught her stealing food from the pantry. Not only was she dirty and hungry, it was obvious she'd been abused."

"Damn. What'd ya do?"

He shrugged. "I fed her and offered her a position in the Galleria kitchen."

Joshua uttered a snort. "Careful, Sam. You might ruin your hard-ass reputation."

"I'll take my chances."

"You think he's really her brother?" Joshua refolded the paper and secured it in the top drawer of his desk.

Sam pinched the bridge of his nose, filled with worry for a young woman he barely knew but felt compelled to help. "The resemblance is there, though I can't know for certain. Until she trusts me enough to confide in me, she'll remain under my protection."

Izzy dried the last breakfast plate, laying it carefully atop the rest. Flipping the damp towel onto her shoulder, she hefted the stack and carried them over to the dish cabinet, settling them inside. Normally somewhat clumsy, she'd been relieved to discover much steadier hands since she began working and living at the Galleria.

The lovely slippers Samuel brought her the other day helped. He'd assured her the cost would come out of her wages in incremental installments until paid off. It had been such a thoughtful gesture Izzy didn't have the heart to refuse.

In a far corner next to the flour bins, Dolores industriously kneaded bread. Izzy wandered over, drawn to the wonderfully yeasty fragrance emanating from the warm dough. "It smells so good, Missus Lund. May I help in any way?"

Her eyes crinkling with a smile, the cook paused mid-knead. "Please, call me Dolores. Do you know how to make corn pone? I should have enough slurry left if you want it to rise."

Izzy nodded eagerly. "I can make a quick pone. My mother had a lovely talent with it. I know how to make it her way. Except she preferred sweet rather than plain."

"You go right ahead, dear girl. I'm fond of sweet things, and I wager our patrons will be, too." She finished shaping the loaf and started on another, punching down the dough. "Everything you need is in the pantry."

Excited to be actually baking instead of scrubbing, Izzy made for the pantry, her mother's recipe ingredients already running through her mind as she gathered a sack of meal and a can of Rumford, thrilled to find molasses to drizzle over the pone once it came out hot and fresh from the oven. Since Luellen Lund, Dolores's adorable daughter, had churned butter earlier in the morning, Izzy would melt a chunk and slather it over the pone, too. Thinking about biting into a piece of the delicious stuff, her mouth watered.

For a while Izzy worked side by side with Dolores, mixing and measuring, their companionable silence broken by conversation and shared laughter. While Dolores began preparing potatoes for boiling, Izzy finished forming her pone rounds. Bent over the cavernous oven, she popped the first large pan inside. She straightened at the sound of boot heels clicking across the floor.

Turning, she nearly stumbled into Samuel. Knowing she must be a mess, Izzy brushed at her untidy hair. "What are you doing here?"

His tense, unsmiling gaze pinned her. Grasping her by the wrist, he pulled her from the kitchen. "Izzy will be back shortly, Dolores," he called over his shoulder.

Izzy tried to keep up with his longer stride and wondered what on earth was going on.

Samuel led her to the same side salon again, shutting the door behind him. He deposited her on the nearest chaise and sat next to her. Izzy inched back. With him still holding her wrist, she couldn't retreat any further.

"What is it?" She hated the tremble in her voice.

Without preamble he asked, "Do you have a brother named Willy?"

A low cry burst from her lips. How did Samuel know her brother's name? She hadn't spoken it, nor had she even alluded to a brother. Her vision actually dimmed as a panicked wheeze sounded in her throat.

"Easy now." Samuel brought his arm around her shoulders and hauled her closer. "It's just you and me." He stroked one hand up and down her arm, the motion oddly soothing. "The family member you spoke of the other night, the one you thought you saw out the window. Who did you think it was, Izzy?"

Her heartbeat thundered in her veins at the implication of how the Galleria's hired peacekeeper could possibly know of her brother's existence. She struggled weakly. Fear knotted her insides and her head swam. "Let me go. I need to go."

"No one's going to hurt you, Izzy. I promise. Calm down and tell me what you're afraid of."

Father's wealth had bought off richer men than Samuel Singleton. Could she trust him? Or would he pass her to her brother, who might kill her for what she'd done?

Or even worse, deposit me back into Father's hands.

Unable to stop the tremors that shook her, a moan fell from her lips.

Samuel tipped up her chin so he could look her directly in the eyes. "Please, don't be afraid. I swear on my life I'll take care of you. But I need to know what has you so frightened."

Sam struggled to tamp down the fury that burned through him like a shot of rotgut. Somehow, he had to convince her to trust him. From the beginning he'd felt responsible for this young woman.

I'll do everything in my power to keep her safe.

"Is Willy your brother?"

Izzy gripped his biceps and buried her face into his chest. Sam tightened his arms around her. "Yes," she whispered against his shirt collar.

"Why are you afraid of him?"

At the sound of light footsteps, Sam glanced toward the door as it swung open and Hannah peeked inside. Sweetheart that she was, she'd probably come to the kitchen to check on her new staff member, and Dolores had told her of his unusual antics. With a shake of his head, he mouthed, "I'll explain later."

Proving her trust in him, Hannah merely nodded, and quietly closed the door.

I'll owe her two buttermilk pies tomorrow. He'd willingly buy her a dozen.

Stroking Izzy's silky curls until her trembling stopped, Sam continued to hold her as another minute passed.

Releasing a stuttering sigh, she eased from his embrace. Sam dropped his arm and waited, hoping she wouldn't try to bolt.

Suspicion clouded her eyes, yet her voice held steady. "How do you know Willy?"

"He came to town earlier, looking for you."

Every drop of color left her face.

Fearful she might swoon, Sam grabbed her elbow to steady her. "It's all right. He'd gone to the jailhouse. Sheriff Lang and I told him we didn't know you, have never seen you. He left town, Izzy. I watched him ride out."

"He left?"

"He did. Now tell me why he scares you."

She pressed her lips together stubbornly. Sam could have cursed aloud in frustration. Knowing it'd only spook her further, he held hard to his dwindling patience. The last thing he wanted to do was make her run again.

She sniffled, unshed tears dampening her lashes. Sam fished a bandana from his pocket and held it out, waiting again while she dabbed at the corners of her eyes. Twisting the soft linen into knots, she rasped, "I believe Father killed my mother."

Sam jerked at her bald statement, feeling his brows climb to his hairline. What on earth could he say to her? Bad enough she lost her mother, and she so young, in need of maternal guidance. Hell, he'd seen how she'd blossomed under the tender care of both Hannah and Dolores, who seemed to adore her already.

Fighting to remain even-tempered, Sam murmured, "I'm sorry about your mother. When did this happen?"

"She disappeared two years ago. Father told me she'd chosen to return East. I don't believe it. My mother loved me, and she'd never leave me by myself with my father and brother."

"Why?"

She dropped her gaze to the carpet runner in front of the chaise. "My father is not a good man."

Not liking where this was headed, Sam resisted the urge to force her to meet his eyes, knowing his anger could only grow stronger. "Did he hurt you?"

"He ignored me, for the most part." Her lower lip trembled. "Until my mother disappeared."

"What did he do then?"

"I became a prisoner of sorts. More like a maid. Then one night, I overheard him talking to Willy. The two of them were plotting to marry me off to one of Father's business associates. Reginald Dalton, a man known for his cruelty and nearly three times my age." A shudder visibly shook her. "Even as a schoolgirl, I sensed his interest in me. I believe he began offering for me years ago."

A low growl erupted from Sam's throat; he couldn't hold it back. "Is that when you ran?"

"No." She fidgeted. Glanced away again. Looked back at him. *Glance away. Look back.* Two fat tears escaped her overflowing lids. "I refused my father's demands to marry this man and was beaten for it. Locked in my room."

"Sonofa—" Sam took hold of her shoulders, barely refraining from pulling her near, afraid he'd frighten the poor girl even more with his urge to track down both her father and brother and pound them bloody. "How did you escape?"

"They starved me for a few days, thinking I'd finally capitulate. So I pretended to agree. Father gave Willy permission to feed me. I heard him coming down the hall with my supper and hid behind the door. When he entered with the tray, I smashed a lamp over his head."

"Smart girl." He dropped a quick kiss onto her forehead. "So, your brother is a bad man, too?"

"Yes."

"Did he abuse you as well?" The thought made his blood boil.

"Not like Father. Willy would slap me sometimes, but he never really hurt me. It was more to humiliate me, I think."

Clamping down on his own urge to hunt down the McDougall men, Sam made a silent vow this sweet young woman would never again have to suffer at their hands. Despising his need to further question her, he set her aside to look for any possible deceit. "Izzy, this is important—"

"I don't want to say anything more." She dropped her gaze.

It actually hurt him to push her for more information, but he had no choice. The more he knew, the better he could guard her and anyone else caught in the crossfire of this situation.

"Izzy, look at me." He waited until she glanced back up. "Your brother gave the sheriff a piece of paper with Silver Cache written on it. He asked for a telegram to be sent to him there if you were spotted anywhere around town. Is Silver Cache where you lived?"

"What does it matter?"

Give me patience. "It matters because we have lawmen in Silver Cache who can watch your folks and report anything suspicious to us. If this rich man who expects to marry you lives there, or if by chance he decides to come here in search of you, the law in Silver Cache can get word to us so we can be ready for him.”

“And then what?” Izzy stared him down. “Reginald is a powerful man, and I have no actual proof he’s cruel, only rumors I heard back in Chicago.”

“Your family is originally from Chicago?”

She nodded. “I can’t return to Silver Cache. If I do, my father will marry me off to Reginald. If you say I’m safe here in town, I believe you. Can’t we just leave it there?”

Her obvious desperation overrode Sam’s need to drag all her secrets out in the open, once and for all. Izzy had already endured so much in her young life. If he continued to push her, he’d lose what small advantage he’d gained.

Forcing away his frustration, Sam rose to his feet and pulled her up beside him. “All right, we’ll leave it be.”

For now.

Chapter 5

Stifling a yawn, Izzy dragged herself down the staff hallway toward the kitchen. A mostly sleepless night left her heavy-eyed and in desperate need of some of Dolores's strong coffee. This early in the morning, however, she might need to grind the beans and then brew it herself. After tossing in her bed most of the night, it seemed pointless to remain in her room when she could be achieving something useful.

Surprised to see the lamps already lit and trimmed inside the pre-sunrise shadows of the kitchen, Izzy plodded over to the stove as Dolores strode in with an armful of linen which she stacked on the table. "Morning, Dolores. You're up very early."

"There you are, dear girl. I was about to knock on your door." She plucked a clean apron off a hook inside the pantry door and held it out. "We'll be busy today. The poker tourney begins and those who participate will want to eat *and* gamble."

Izzy fastened her apron and smoothed the hem down to cover her uniform. "What should I do first?"

Dolores bustled around the kitchen, pulling out pots and pitchers, passing them to Izzy who followed to collect each item. "Go ahead and set everything on the counters, there's a love. Patsy's staying at the Stage House today, so Trudy Parsons will be coming to help out. You haven't met her yet. A darling child. Married to our Ben, one of Sheriff Lang's deputies. Such a hard worker, like you." She winked at Izzy.

Warmth infused her at the compliment. In the week she'd been assisting Dolores, Izzy hoped her very best would be good enough for the often insanely busy Galleria kitchen. "Thank you, Dolores. I do love working here."

"Well, we love having you." Dolores paused in her whirlwind trek, studying everything from icebox to pantry. "Coffee, and plenty of it." Before Izzy could heartily agree, Dolores poked at a covered bowl. "Blast. We only have three dozen eggs, which isn't enough. Have you ever collected from a laying hen?" She plucked a basket off its hook. "Right down the back path from the Galleria, you'll find Sheriff Lang's house. You met Vivian Lang already, didn't you?"

At her hesitant nod, Dolores beamed. "Excellent. Vivian supplies us with extra eggs from her hens. It would help greatly if you'd run over there and collect what you can." She thrust out the basket, lined with several dishcloths. "White house, gray shutters. Flower boxes at the windows. You can't miss it. I'll make you a nice breakfast when you return, all right? Off you go." She flapped her apron teasingly, and Izzy found herself scurrying out the back door with the large basket hanging off one arm, while sunrise painted the sky a deep rose.

As she walked along, enjoying the cool morning air, Izzy hoped to heaven she wasn't about to wake anyone up in the Lang household, especially Sheriff Lang, whom she'd yet to formally meet. She knew a lady as kind as Vivian would not tie herself to a harsh, unforgiving man nor would she love a lawman whose handsome exterior hid any sort of dishonesty or ill-repute.

Up ahead, the Lang residence came into view, exactly as Dolores had described. Reassured someone was awake by the soft glow of lamplight in two front windows, Izzy approached the wide, inviting porch. If her luck held, it would be Vivian instead of the sheriff.

As she neared, the front door opened and Vivian peeked out with a welcoming smile. "Izzy, what a lovely surprise." Her gaze dropped to the basket. "Dolores sacrificed you for egg-gathering, I see."

"Sacrifice?" That didn't sound promising.

"I'm teasing, silly. My hens are very well-behaved." Vivian pushed the door wider.

Izzy entered, spying the babe cuddled against one lilac-covered shoulder. "Oh, how precious."

Vivian nuzzled the downy head. "This is my son, Isiah." She gestured for Izzy to follow her into a cozy sitting room. "He fell asleep while I nursed, so I'll lay him down and he should be fine for a few hours or so. Maybe."

She nestled her son into a low wooden cradle, covering him with a soft quilt. Taking a seat on a nearby settee, she tucked bare feet beneath her dressing gown. "Nate—he's our oldest—spends three days a week during the summer out at the Carter Mine, tutoring some of the younger children." She slowly rocked the cradle. "How are you faring at the Galleria? I have been so busy around here, I've not had a chance to check on you."

Izzy had been watching the babe in its cradle as he squirmed and fretted, finally relaxing into sleep. *Someday, I want one of those.*

She hadn't realized she'd murmured aloud until Vivian spoke. "Well, certainly you do. Once you find the right gentleman to assist you."

"Oh, Lord." Mortified, Izzy sank onto the nearest chair, the basket now abandoned to the polished slat floor. "I sure didn't mean to imply anything—"

"Of course not." Vivian shoved her hair, gathered into a loose braid, over one shoulder. "You are of marriageable age. You should be thinking of finding yourself a fellow and settling down. Little Creede is a wonderful place to live."

"I'm sure it is," Izzy demurred, wondering how to extricate herself from a conversation rapidly becoming uncomfortable. She poked at her apron, ruffling the edges, smoothing them down. "I have only been here a week and . . ." She swallowed against a throat gone suddenly dry. "Only a week."

If she stayed, it would mean this wonderful town had somehow become safe for her. If she left, it would be against the threat of Father or Willy coming for her. *I'll never live under their thumbs again.*

She met Vivian's compassionate gaze with a forced smile. "Shall you point me in the direction of those well-behaved hens? Missus Dolores might send a search party out for me if I tarry any longer."

Sam rested his arms on the second-floor railing, assessing the herd of gents swarming the front receiving parlor. A fast head count assured this poker tourney surpassed January's event which had brought in participants from as far away as Georgetown, the harsher winter travel having no effect on a hard-core gambling man.

With Harrison Carter's approval, Sam had pulled in several of the younger miners to help with the tourney, from registration to gaming control, peacekeeping, and overall muscle where needed. His experiences, with past tourneys in other places, had resulted in a list of what not to do. He'd learned a pretty woman dressed a certain way might bring in many eager players, but also caused more trouble than those additional gamblers might be worth once the liquor started flowing heavily and the men's veneer of civility dropped.

Behind the counter, Caleb Washburn recorded names and betting totals, while his brother John collected purses and doled out equivalences in the blue, white, and black-painted chips Knight had imported from *Belle Joleen,* the riverboat he'd owned and sold before moving West to Colorado. Sam noticed a few of the older men protested turning over their money purses for safekeeping, yet the serious, steady John only had to touch his sidearm for them to back down and comply. The Washburns were tall, broad-shouldered, strapping young men. Sam had already approached both regarding future employment at the Galleria, once their university studies back East were finished.

A subtle, flowery scent teased his nostrils as Hannah joined him at the railing. Turned out impeccably in a loose, ruffled gown the exact color of her pink cheeks, she indicated the organized chaos below with her usual calm. "Well, Mister Samuel, what do you think? More this time around, I'd reckon. Shall I send for additional whiskey and bourbon?"

Impressed at the way those two very manly words rolled with ease off her ladylike tongue, Sam replied somberly, "I think we'll be fine." He sent her a wink, amused when she returned it with one of her own. "Missus Hannah, you are indeed the First Lady of the Galleria."

She straightened the edges of her shawl. "Of course I am. It's my sworn duty."

Sam remained at her side, content to keep her company and in idle chat, yet finding his mind wandering to Izzy as it had often done in the past few days. After their conversation and what she revealed the other morning, he'd only seen her once or twice in brief passing. Each time, an endearing blush attested to her discomfort over the information she'd shared. He didn't want to make the woman leery of him and was determined not to push her.

Until I have no choice.

As if to mock his oath, a familiar figure wended through the thinning crowd of registrants. At the counter he removed his feathered bowler and shoved it under his arm, his mop of curly dark hair easily recognizable.

Willy McDougall, thinking to join the tourney? Sam scoffed at the notion. He'd lay money the man plotted to snoop around Little Creede until he found his sister.

He caught Hannah's arm and led her away from the railing. "Where's Izzy?"

Her eyes searched his thoroughly. To her credit, she recognized the seriousness of the situation. "She's in danger."

"Yes, unless I can get her out of here."

"She would still be in the kitchen with Dolores. Take her out to the Carter ranch. Retta could use the help anyway, as close as she is to delivering. Izzy will be safe there as long as you're not spotted going out of town." As she spoke Hannah pushed him down the second-floor hall toward the back staircase leading directly to the kitchen. "Don't waste time packing her a bag, Samuel. Just take her away for now."

Sweating, dressed in a pair of trousers and a hunting coat borrowed from Vivian's son, a hat pulled down over her forehead, Izzy bent low over Tinker's back. The big stallion, on loan from Joshua's stable, flew like the wind and easily kept up with the beautiful paint mare Samuel rode.

Finding out she could fit into boys' clothing—one barely ten years old, no less—proved to be advantageous as well as downright humiliating. After dragging her out of the Galleria kitchen and urging her down the path back to Vivian's house, Samuel had shared the unsettling news her brother was on the prowl for her.

Izzy's legs had trembled as her stomach knotted. "How? Where did you see him?"

"I recognized him when he registered along with all the other poker tourney participants at the Galleria. He didn't see me, Izzy. I'm taking you out of town to a safe place, but first we've got to disguise you, in case your father is also wandering around, too."

At the Lang house, Vivian had listened to Samuel's hurried explanation of why he needed Nate's clothing. "I've just the thing," she assured, and had hustled Izzy into what appeared to be a boy's room. Opening a bureau drawer, she dug out the trousers, adding the coat and even a pair of heavy socks. "Pull these over your pretty slippers to protect them," she'd instructed. "We'll stash your dress in a saddlebag. You'll borrow one of our horses, too. Sam can saddle Tinker."

Now Izzy clung to the stallion, the hot midday sun beating on her head, as they took the back trails on the way to the spread of ranches owned by Vivian's brothers, Frank and Harrison. She would be safe there, Vivian had promised. No one would find her, not with all the men on guard since the land itself abutted the Carter Mine and village.

Only a few days ago she'd dismissed the thought her family would come for her. Even after Samuel had told her of Willy's visit to the sheriff, she'd still remained certain he wouldn't return, nor would Father care enough to try and find her.

I should have known better. Without her, they'd be forced to cook and clean for themselves. Bitterness coated her tongue at the thought.

Ahead, Samuel reined his mare to an easy canter, following a partial tree line, and Izzy pulled herself from her misery enough to take in her surroundings. Birdsong and bubbling water blended, an occasional lowing providing harmony. Lush pasture spread out, dotted with sheep and goats on one side of the trail and cattle on the other. The trail widened, offering views of a sprawling ranch framed with a split log fence and an enormous cottonwood boasting a swing made of planks and thick rope. In the distance sat a beautiful cabin, along with other assorted buildings.

"Frank Carter's old place." Samuel gestured toward the cabin. "Built it himself and used to live there. Once he married Catherine and moved to town, the Carter Mine's new foreman took it over."

Samuel swung off his horse and stepped to her side, holding Tinker's halter. "Ready?"

Izzy hesitated, her gaze shifting to the house. "I—" She cleared a lump from her throat. "I'm not sure about this."

She didn't know these people, though she'd heard only good things about them from both Hannah and Vivian.

"The Carters are trustworthy folk." He helped her dismount. "I'd never do anything to put you in danger."

Taking him at his word, she swung her leg over the stallion's back, gasping when her sock caught in the stirrup and sent her tumbling forward. Samuel easily caught her in his strong arms as Nate's hat slipped off her head. With her feet barely touching the ground, he held her against his hard body.

Izzy shook her curls out of the way and met Samuel's gaze. "Thank you."

His lips curved briefly as he set her firmly on her feet. He snatched up the hat and dropped it back on her head. "At your service, Miss Izzy." Holding her by her elbow, he led her up the stone path toward the ranch house. "Harrison and Retta Carter live here. This is the safest place you could be right now, I promise."

No sooner were the words out of his mouth, than a towheaded girl, all gangly legs and arms, tore around the side of the house, brandishing a stick almost as tall as she was. "Halt, varmint," she yelled, "or I'll run you through!" Skidding to a stop several feet away, she flipped a tangled plait of hair over her shoulder and squinted in the sun. "Mister Sam?"

While Izzy gaped, Samuel doffed his hat and bowed low. "It's me, you heathen. Where's your ma?"

"In with the hogs." The girl swung on a grubby heel and ran back around the side of the house, hollering, "Mama, Mister Sam and some boy just rode up."

Chuckling, Samuel gently squeezed Izzy's elbow. "Welcome to Bedlam."

Chapter 6

Scowling, Joshua slapped the telegram on his desk. His hard gaze met Sam's. "Izzy McDougall's father is the nephew of Roger Jennings, on the mother's side."

The name rang familiar to Sam. "I've heard of him, here and there over the years. Notorious as hell."

"Yep. From a crime family out of Chicago. Been at it for over two decades. Ran everything from brothels to crooked billiards and faro gaming."

Sam frowned in concentration as his recollection with some of the history came back to him. "Wasn't he also accused of extortion and murder?"

"Nothing was ever proven. Jennings moved to the East coast about five years ago. I understand his children took his place. Others in his underworld drifted West."

At the thought of Izzy being dragged back into a family related to people like that, Sam's blood curdled. "You think Izzy's father is currently involved in criminal activity?"

"I do. Rumor is his son shot a man in the head for taking intimacies with one of his lady loves." Joshua's nostrils flared, eyes narrowing. "Evidently Willy retaliated by brutalizing the woman before forcing her into prostitution, where she was later killed by a customer."

"No charges were brought against him?"

"There wasn't anyone willing to stand against the younger McDougall in court, for fear of bringing Jennings's wrath down on their families." Joshua poked at the telegram. "I saw enough of this criminal element on my travels to understand the mindset of those unwilling witnesses. It's why this level of crime has been able to catch a foothold especially in large cities."

"Hell." Sam dropped into one of Joshua's visiting chairs. "And Izzy's father?"

"Deeply involved. Back in the day, his own father, William McDougall the Second was an attorney for two of the crime families. William McDougall the Third joined up as an attorney after graduating from the most prestigious law academy in the state."

Sam quirked a brow. "Let me guess. Willy is William McDougall the Fourth and destined to carry on the legacy of crooked law dealings."

"You'd be right. Some poking around in Silver Cache might be a good idea." Joshua rubbed his chin thoughtfully. "Matter of fact, Robert Blackwood is the new sheriff in Silver Cache these days. You recall, he resettled there right after he married Gleason's niece."

At the mention of Magnolia Sanders—now Blackwood—Sam allowed a faint smile. The couple had married on a Sunday and rode out of town three days later. "I recall. Never seen a man so happy to be shackled."

"I'll send word to Robert, see what he knows. He's got a knack for prying without anyone even knowing they're being investigated."

"Appreciate it, Lang." Sam's smile faded as he pondered the rest of his disquiet. "I have another name I'd like you to check out. Reginald Dalton, also from the Chicago area." Joshua sent him a questioning glance and Sam spat out, "The man is determined to marry Izzy, and her father promised he could have her."

"That why she ran?"

"Partly. When she refused to marry Dalton, her father beat her and locked her in her room." Anger tightened Sam's muscles. "Can't verify for sure until I fully gain her trust, but I doubt it was her first beating."

"What makes you say that?"

"Her skittishness, for one. The way she sizes up every man she meets as if trying to determine if he's a threat." He shrugged, begrudgingly offering some insight into his own past. "I'm keenly aware of the signs of abuse."

At Joshua's raised brows, Sam admitted, "I grew up in a strict orphanage. Got tossed there when I was about Addie Carter's age. Children in those places get pounded on a lot for no reason other than they exist and are fair game for bullies."

Memories of children crying because they'd wet their beds, which always brought on harsh retaliation, filled Sam's mind along with the echo of mean slaps, a paddle, even a belt whistling through the air, slashing down over their narrow backs. He'd been too small to stop the headmaster from administering punishment, no matter how hard he'd tried. Once, Sam had grabbed on to the man's britches, trying to slow him down, only to be thrown over the bannister, breaking an arm in two places and one of his legs.

"Tough way to grow up, Singleton." Joshua got to his feet and came around the side of his desk. "I'd hate to see a young, innocent woman made to suffer a similar fate." He snatched his hat off the desk and plopped it on his head. "I'll head over to the telegraph office right away and I'll be sure to include this Dalton gent in the message."

"I'll walk with you." Sam hesitated, then thought *what the hell.* "I traveled some after I got out on my own. Spent time up and down the Mississippi, on riverboats and in larger cities. Now and then someone I'd meet, let's just say on the more disreputable side, would mention the Jennings family. I wouldn't be surprised to find out Dalton is in with the bunch as well."

As he followed the sheriff out the door he added, "I have some *not-so-upstanding* acquaintances I can contact, too."

Lang groaned. "Don't want to know about that."

"Addie," Retta called out to her precocious eldest child, "stop running in the house. Take Noodle and your sister and go outside. Don't go far, the boys will be waking up shortly, and I'll need you both to help me feed them."

Izzy watched the girl come to a screeching halt near the kitchen door. "All right, Mama." She spun around and raced back the way she'd come, calling, "Jenny, don't be a slowpoke." With the dog nipping playfully at her heels, Addie flung open the half-door, her three-year-old sister in fast pursuit. The girls and galloping beagle disappeared around the corner as the door slowly swung shut.

"I swear, those two never slow down." Retta indicated her protruding belly. "This one's been acting up quite a bit lately, too. Lord help us. Once she arrives, I don't think Harrison and I will ever sleep again."

"You think it's a girl?"

"I do." Retta caressed the pronounced bump, lowering her head as if speaking to the babe inside. "You in a hurry to come out, little one?" She offered Izzy a blinding smile. "This child's on the move. Would you like to feel her?"

"Oh my," Izzy exclaimed in awe, "you wouldn't mind?"

"Of course not." Retta took Izzy's hand and placed it on her stomach. "There. Feel it?"

"Yes." Amazed at the fluttering beneath her hand, Izzy met Retta's beaming gaze. For a full minute she remained at Retta's side, enchanted, as the unborn babe kicked energetically. "She's so active in there."

"She is," Retta agreed, carefully settling on a kitchen chair draped in a thick blanket. She fanned herself. "Harrison insists I sit on this danged thing to help cushion my hips. I swear it's like perching over a banked fire in this heat."

Izzy sat across from her. "He's worried about you, I'm sure." It had not escaped her notice how pale Retta appeared, compared to Hannah Gleason's robust constitution and rosy complexion during her confinement. "Is everything all right?"

"Oh, I'm doing as well as can be expected, I suppose. It will be my fourth delivery, and I became with child fairly quickly after the twins' birth." Retta's blush sent faint pink clear to her hairline. "Didn't mean to be indelicate."

"You're not, truly," Izzy hastened to assure her. "I understand the rudiments of childbearing, and I confess to anticipating my own experiences." Now it was her turn to flush hot. "If I ever marry, that is."

"Surely, you'll marry. Goodness knows there are plenty of fine men around here."

"So Vivian says," Izzy replied, amused.

"A wise young woman, our Vivian. I don't believe Joshua stood a chance against her." She inhaled sharply. "Ouch. Our lass might be dancing in there. I had better walk a bit." She made to rise, then sat down abruptly. "Perhaps not."

"What's wrong?" Izzy asked.

"A bit of dizziness. It will pass. The last time I had this problem, Doc Sheaton's wife showed me some breathing exercises." Retta inhaled and exhaled, blowing out evenly. "I tended to get dizzy at times with my girls. The twins never gave me a moments' trouble until their birth, the little rascals." After another deep breath, she rested her head against the back of the chair. "There, now. Already feeling better."

Izzy wasn't so sure. "Maybe I should go find your husband."

"No need to alarm Harrison. I promise I'm fine. Though, if someone were to cut me a piece of elderberry pie," Retta said with sudden mischief, gesturing toward the counter where a covered dish sat, "I sure wouldn't mind a bit."

One elbow resting on the bar at his back, Sam focused his attention on the poker game underway at table nine as he tossed back a shot of whiskey. After almost two days of nonstop gaming, scowls and ribald comments indicated the players' rising tensions. Although guns were required to be surrendered at the door, he knew at least a few of the men would have managed to smuggle in a weapon. Tempted to throw back another shot, Sam thought better of it, knowing he needed his wits about him.

Walker, a gambler from Kansas City who had a reputation as a card cheat, took a long draw of his cigar, releasing it slowly into the smoky room. He tossed a stack of chips in the center. "I'm in."

His amused gaze swept over the grumbling men as they threw their cards down. Mumbles of "I'm out," and "Too rich for me," ringed the table. All except the stranger who'd moseyed in an hour earlier. The man had a hard edge about him Sam didn't trust, and he'd been losing for most of the game.

Sam had been around enough gambling houses in his past to know trouble when he saw it. Straightening, he set the shot glass on the bar and made his way toward the table. The snappy tune of 'Oh! Susanna' sang in the air from Thaddeus's piano. He'd been playing for hours.

Leaning forward in his chair, the stranger stared at Walker as if he could read his cards, sight unseen. "Call," he gritted out, settling back and pushing his chips onto the growing pile.

Walker grinned, adding more chips. "Call."

Without taking his eyes off Walker, the stranger slowly splayed out his cards. "Aces over."

Walker spread his own hand on the table. "All red, queen high." He swept out an arm and dragged the considerable mound of chips toward him.

With a growl, the stranger reached under his vest but froze when Sam nudged the muzzle of his Colt to the back of his head. "I wouldn't do that."

The poker tables went silent, and the music trailed off with a tinkle of discordant notes as every eye locked on the stranger currently chewing over what few options he had. Either he backed down, or Sam would shoot him. Since cleaning up the mess would delay the games for at least an hour, he hoped the man would choose wisely.

Finally, the stranger's posture relaxed, and he eased back into his seat, resting his arms on the table. "He's cheating."

The danger now past, Thaddeus struck up a new tune and the rest of the tables resumed their games.

Sam uncocked his Colt. "Maybe, maybe not." He glanced over at Walker. "You cheatin'?"

"No, sir," he replied with a smirk.

Sam arched a brow in disbelief at the denial but maintained a bland expression as he turned back to the stranger. "Well, there you have it." He eased to the side so he could meet the stranger's glare. "If you wanna stay, you're gonna need to turn your gun in, right over there." He nodded toward the front where Smiley Boone, one of the Carter miners employed for the tourney, stood ready to collect his weapon.

Scowling, the angry gambler stood. "I can find better games in Georgetown." He stomped toward the door.

By the time Sam returned his attention to the table, the stranger's chair had already been claimed as a new set began.

He took up his position at the bar to stand watch.

The next few hours passed in relative calm, until Izzy's brother walked into the tourney salon. Tension flooded Sam as McDougall scanned the room and spotted him. With an ugly sneer, the man closed the distance between them in three angry strides.

Sam flipped back his coat, his Colt now easily accessible, and tamped down his fury. He wanted to beat Izzy's brother within an inch of his life for hurting her.

As if sensing trouble, the room once again quieted. Willy McDougall stopped an arm's length away. Sam watched him dispassionately, poised for action, waiting.

McDougall showed his teeth menacingly. "Why'd you lie to me, Singleton?"

Sam bit back a curse. "Don't know what you're talking about." *Figured out his sister was in town, I'd lay money.*

"Where is she?"

"Where's who?" The bastard wasn't going to get his hooks into Izzy. *Ever.*

"My sister," Willy spat.

"Like I said, haven't seen her." The lie came easily as the urge to pull his weapon and shoot nearly overwhelmed him. His trigger finger twitched above his pistol.

McDougall's gaze narrowed. "Bullshit. I talked to folks around town, and they say she's working here."

Sam shrugged. "They're wrong."

"You think you're so smart." McDougall shot a glare around the salon. "What the hell're you all looking at?"

No one moved, except to openly watch the show. A few chuckles echoed here and there.

Red-faced, McDougall's hate-filled stare locked on Sam. "You got no right to keep my sister away from her family. She's to be wed, you know. As soon as I report this to her betrothed, we'll be back to collect her."

Sam itched to tell the bastard Izzy didn't belong to anyone, but that'd give away the fact he did indeed know her, so he kept his mouth shut.

"This ain't the end, Singleton." Willy spun on his boot heel and stormed out of the salon. Sam took relieved note of how Ben discreetly followed. The deputy would make sure the idiot left town.

With the entertainment over, the games picked up at each table. In the adjoining salon, Gleason's roulette wheel spun and clacked.

Sam waited a short minute, then strode over to the side window in time to see McDougall heading for the coach station. Abner Dale manned the station by himself, dealing with stage scheduling and mailbags when he wasn't working the telegraph equipment. Abner'd send anything in a telegram and never question its wording.

Was Willy contacting his father? Or Reginald Dalton back East?

Either one wasn't good.

He turned to Smiley. "Keep an eye on things for a bit. Washburn's manning the front desk. Get him to help out if you need to."

"Sure thing."

Five minutes later, Sam walked into the Sheriff's office at the jailhouse, surprised to find Robert Blackwood talking with Lang. He shook the man's hand. "I thought you and your lovely lady were still in Silver Cache. You got my telegram?"

"Yep. We were packed to travel anyway, headed back to see how Hannah's doing." He leaned a hip on the desk. "Tell me what's going on."

Sam removed his hat and slapped it against his thigh. "Do you know a William McDougall from Silver Cache? Older fellow, an attorney who came out from Chicago."

"Matter of fact, I do," Robert replied. "As I was telling Joshua, I think he's dirty."

Joshua sat back in his chair. "Sam, did you know Izzy's brother Willy's back in town?"

Sam frowned. "He came into the Galleria looking for her. Said he knew she worked there and wanted to know why I lied."

"What'd you tell him?" Joshua asked.

"Lied some more. Told him he was mistaken and he left." He encompassed both men in the conversation. "Saw him go into the telegraph office. Ben's following him. Let's hope Willy's only contacting his father."

Robert looked confused. "Only?"

Sam nodded grimly. "We might be able to keep her out of her father's clutches, at least for a while. But if he's sending word to Reginald Dalton, and he comes to collect her himself, things could get dicey."

"I recall you asking about that name in your telegram," Robert mused. "Why?"

Joshua answered for him. "Because Dalton is supposedly her betrothed."

"She's unwilling, believe me," Sam growled. "Wants nothing to do with the old son of a bitch."

Joshua studied the broadside calendar Territorial Prison sent out along with the usual *wanted* posters. "It'll take him at least two weeks' travel from Chicago, depending on how often coaches run from Georgetown."

"That allows for some time to—"

Robert cleared his throat. "Gentleman. I'm sorry to say, Dalton arrived by coach in Silver Cache several days ago."

Sam scraped his hand over his hair. "Damnation."

"Does this woman mean something to you, Sam?" Robert asked.

"No. I mean, yes. Maybe . . ."

His voice trailed off, his gut clenching at the thought of sweet Izzy being forced into a marriage with a man who'd hurt her. "Hell yes, she means something to me."

"All right then." Robert picked up his hat, smoothing out the brim, meeting Sam's frown with one of his own. "Look, Singleton. If you care about her, the only way to keep her safe is to marry her yourself."

Chapter 7

"Singleton." Willy paced the parlor floor. "I know he's got her hidden somewhere in that gambling saloon."

Willy watched in disgust as his father swayed on his feet, the snifter in his loose grip sloshing its contents down the front of his vest.

The old man harrumphed and eyed him blearily, raising another brandy to his lips. Thin red veins crawled across his broad nose and cheeks, the aftereffect of too much to drink. "I told you to do some digging around during the tourney. Perfect opportunity and all."

"With Singleton and the hired muscle that Irish bastard owner has slinking all over the place, I couldn't break away," Willy snapped, fed up with his drunken sire. "I'll have to go back and get into another game. Maybe roulette this time." He slapped his palms together in anticipation. "Now, there's a game for a gentleman—"

"Which you, unfortunately, are not," came the sarcastic response from across the shadowed room. Reginald Dalton moved into the firelight, the glow from its orange banked coals throwing his craggy features into stark relief. Tall, distinguished, his salt-and-pepper hair combed precisely, Dalton wore the trappings of his wealth with ease.

Beneath the expensive clothes and worldly air, a beast lived, a sadist who enjoyed torture. Animals, the lower class, women . . . he took delight in any downtrodden soul unlucky enough to come under his whip.

Willy refused to waste time pondering the damage his sister would have to endure, in and out of the marriage bed. Men owned their women, and once they were wed and out of the house, all responsibility for their wellbeing ceased.

Besides, after Father, drunk and more loose-lipped than usual one night, spilled his secrets, Willy knew they had no choice. The next morning, Dalton had commenced his blackmail.

The man could send both Willy and his father to the nearest prison if he didn't get what he wanted.

My sister.

Dalton lifted his fancy boiled-wool Homburg from a side table. A diamond stickpin decorated his left lapel, glinting in the low lamplight. In this summer heat, he still wore the embroidered vest and tailored coat he'd arrived in four days ago. Willy wondered if the stuffed shirt took it off at bedtime.

Time to establish some rank around here. "I'm rejoining the tourney tomorrow, Mister Dalton." It galled Willy to keep politeness in his tone. "I'll find Isadora—"

"You couldn't find your own ass," Dalton retorted. He leaned intimidatingly closer, the smell of his expensive hair pomade nauseating. "I'll be going with you. Register for any game you want. Just keep the muscle off my tail until I can find my wayward bride-to-be."

Izzy stood on the porch, enjoying the peaceful morning, when a cold, wet nose rooted at her bare foot. "Silly dog." She dropped to her knees to ruffle Noodle's fur, grinning at the crazed wagging tail and wriggling back end of the overly affectionate beagle. Never having been allowed the comfort of a pet, she found herself enamored by Noodle, as well as Addie's cat Dobby, a nighttime cuddler able to shake the bed with her purrs. Since she'd arrived at the ranch, she hadn't slept by herself, awakening in the dark with either or both devoted animals lying next to her for at least a part of the night.

"She likes ya." Jenny plopped down on the top stoop, her wrinkled pinafore raising a small dust cloud. Tangled hair the color of chocolate fell in clumps over her shoulder, pieces of twigs caught in the silky strands. "Don't let her lick ya, 'cause she licks her hiney somethin' awful," the girl confided.

"I'll make sure to keep that smelly tongue away from me," Izzy vowed, charmed by the Carters' youngest girl. She swiped a gob of mud from Jenny's upturned nose. "How'd you get so dirty? Your mama dressed you in clean clothes not even an hour ago."

Jenny's wide grin revealed tiny milk teeth. "Wanted t' see how the piggies root." She imitated the action, snorting into her palms until Izzy couldn't hold back her laughter. Jenny rubbed at her cheek. "Mighta got too close t' their slop."

"Oh, goodness." Izzy stood hastily, pulling Jenny to her feet. "We'd best wash you up right now. No telling what disgusting things are in there."

"It's stuff we didn't eat the other day, an' some bad taters Mama got outta the cellar." Jenny skipped alongside Izzy as they rounded the house and headed toward the back door. "Pigs don't get sick eatin' it."

"Yes, well, we are not pigs." Izzy hustled Jenny along, picking leaves out of her hair. "Some of us, that is."

In the kitchen, she got a good look at Jenny's feet and halted her progress any further. "You stay on the rug." Crossing the spotless floor, Izzy fetched a rag and pumped water to dunk it in. Returning to the child, she wiped her down while Jenny kept up a mostly-garbled, hysterical monologue on the comings and goings of the ranch, her 'poopy-bottom' brothers, and what might have put a big bump in her mama's tummy.

"I think it's a hooty-owl in there," Jenny finished matter-of-factly.

Izzy paused in scrubbing Jenny's filthy leg. "A hooty-owl?" *Do I really want to know?*

"Yep, 'cause once I heard 'hooty-hooty' in Mama an' Papa's room. Mama told us she was gonna give us somethin' soon, an' Addie told *me* we're gonna get what we want a whole lot, an' I want a hooty-owl." Jenny lifted her leg and inspected it. "All clean."

Izzy blinked at the precocious girl. "How old are you again?"

Jenny held up four fingers. "Mostly this."

"Hmm. Go find another dress so I can soak this one, all right?" Izzy stood, flushing to think anyone might sound like an owl during intimate moments.

"All right, Auntie Izzy." Jenny ran off, leaving Izzy with a fist clenched over her heart, emotional at being referred to as 'auntie.'

She carried the rag to the sink and pumped more water into the dishpan, adding in a small chunk of soap, while childish voices echoed down the hallway where the bedrooms were. Retta habitually spent her mornings working on the twins' refusal to use the potty, with Addie either helping her mother or trying to keep Jenny out of trouble.

Izzy finished wringing out the rag and draped it over a hook as the kitchen door opened and Harrison entered.

He sniffed the air. "Morning. Who got into the pigsty?"

"Is it that obvious?" She bent to pick up the rug. "Maybe I should shake this outside."

"No, I'm only teasing you. I don't smell anything. Jenny met me at the gate in her bloomers and informed me she learned how to root for slop." Harrison toed off his boots, his eyes dancing with mirth. "Not the first time she's played around the piglet pen."

"Aren't you worried the hogs might hurt her?" Izzy poured him a cup of coffee from the pot Retta had left warming on the stove.

He accepted it with a murmur of thanks. "She stays with the young'uns, doesn't go near the hogs. Those piglets are pretty appealing. You ought to go over and see them while you're here." He regarded Izzy keenly, until she wanted to squirm on her seat. "Retta tells me you won't leave the front porch. There's no one who can hurt you out here, Miss McDougall. No one knows where you are."

"Please, call me Izzy. And I don't mean to act like a scaredy cat, truly. It's just—" She shrugged helplessly, not knowing what to say to this big, brawny man who held such sway over half the town, ran a profitable mine firmly yet kindly, and melted like butter around his wife and children.

She'd only met Harrison's brother, Frank Carter, once. He struck her as a somewhat rougher version of his younger sibling. With a wife and child of his own, however, Frank might be as tenderhearted with his family.

Will I ever find someone like that?

An image of Samuel Singleton crossed her mind so swiftly, so clearly, she actually gasped aloud.

"Are you feeling poorly?" Harrison set down his cup and started to rise.

"No, I'm perfectly fine," she began, interrupted by a sharp, ringing cry.

"Harrison, come quickly!"

He jumped to his feet and strode down the hall toward the bedrooms, Izzy following worriedly, only to stop short at the doorway as Harrison rushed inside. "Retta, what's wrong?"

She stood in the center of the room, clutching her distended belly. Izzy gasped to see a spreading puddle of water—mixed with blood—under her feet. In the corner Addie huddled with Jenny and their brothers, the younger children crying softly as she tried to calm them.

"Harrison, it's too soon—" Retta doubled over as Harrison sprang to her side and swept her carefully into his arms, carrying her to the bed. "There shouldn't be blood," she wailed against his shoulder.

"It's going to be all right, sweetheart. Doc'll come."

Izzy hurried to his side as he held Retta's hands. "What can I do?"

"Did Sam show you where Frank used to live?"

"Yes."

Harrison blew out a heavy breath. "Good. Take one of the horses. My foreman lives there now. Elby North. Tell him you're staying with us. He can ride to town for Doc Sheaton. Ask for Elby's wife, too. She midwifes up at the mine village for us when there's a need. Bea will know what to do. Can you do that, Izzy?"

"Yes. Yes, I can." Izzy ran from the room and down the hallway to the front door. As she rounded the house and sped toward the stable, she heard Harrison's comforting rumble and Addie's shaky response. Though the girl was only six, Izzy had no doubt she'd hold up.

Rushing inside the stable, she saddled the first horse she spotted, an enormous reddish stallion who snorted as she approached. "You're such a good boy," she crooned, earning herself a brief snuffle as she swung into the saddle and guided him out of the stable. "Let's go get help."

Chapter 8

The fading notes of "Daisy Deane" floated in from the front parlor as Sam descended the stairs. He'd had to round up some men to move Thaddeus's piano out of the poker salon when Knight announced the need for more tables in there. By the number of gents tapping their toes as they awaited a spot to play, nobody seemed to mind having their conversations interrupted by music.

Weariness settled on Sam's shoulders, the result of a sleepless night thinking about the conversation he'd had at the jailhouse with Robert Blackwood.

Izzy's family problems weren't about to go away anytime soon, and neither would her brother's accusations. Sam wouldn't put it past Willy to drag not only William the Third to Little Creede, but also Dalton, in a bid to force his hand and Izzy's.

Not a chance.

He needed to get out to the ranch as soon as his shift was over. Needed to sit Izzy down and bring home to her the urgency of the situation. Especially after what he'd learned from Blackwood about Dalton's political reach which could easily include a judge or two.

Determined to finish his rounds and see the gaming floor adequately covered, Sam approached the roulette salon and clapped Ben Parsons on the shoulder. The quiet deputy had been standing guard at the entrance. "I might have to leave shortly, Ben. If you can stay longer, maybe grab Dub over at the Stage House to help out, I'd appreciate it."

"You bet," Ben replied easily. "It's been quiet, for the most part. Couple of fools caught cheating. Mister Gleason happened to be here at the time and escorted them out. By the scruff." Ben straightened from the wall where he'd been leaning, rubbing the back of his own neck. "That's one intimidating man when he gets his Irish up."

"You would be right." Sam scanned the room, seeing nothing untoward. Men stood two-deep around the roulette wheel, placing bets, taunting each other, yelling every time someone won and booing when they lost. "Looks like a decent crowd—ah, damn." He dropped one hand to his gun, nodding toward a gap in the roulette table. "How long has the man in the brown suit been here?"

Ben shrugged. "Maybe an hour. Wait a minute. Isn't that the McDougall fella? I spotted him earlier, wanderin' around. Shoulda taken more notice then, but I had to break up a fight in the faro room." He started forward. "I'll run him off."

Sam caught his arm. "No, I've got a few things to say to him. Where'd you see him wander?"

"Stuck his nose in a few doors. Probably nothin', come to think of it."

Maybe. Maybe not. "Stay here." Adjusting his holster, Sam silently wound his way through the crowd, positioning himself behind Willy McDougall, intent on stacking his chips. Waiting until he placed another bet, Sam tapped him on the shoulder. "McDougall, I see you couldn't stay away."

To his credit, Willy maintained a calm mien. "I've come for my sister. Told you I'd be back."

"I believe you told me this *ain't over*, to use your exact words." He glanced at the chips clustered in front of McDougall's seat. "You're doing well for yourself, aren't you? My congratulations." He held McDougall's eyes, noting the sweat rolling down the side of his jaw. "I understand you've been interested in wandering. Opening doors. Poking around."

Fresh perspiration broke out on Willy's upper lip, yet he managed a sneer. "Don't know what you mean." He stood and edged away from the table and his stack of chips.

Sam blocked him. "Oh, I think you know what I mean. You were seen being nosy. Mind telling me what you're looking for?"

"You know what I'm lookin' for, you sumbitch." Willy's fists came up as he widened his stance in an attempt to appear imposing. "Isadora's in town, probably right in this fancy building."

Sam tapped his thumb against the Colt on his hip. "If you've lost her, that's your problem. *My* immediate concern would be the reason you think it's acceptable to snoop around our gambling establishment during a tourney where large sums of money are held. Protected. Or maybe you think your curiosity might get you a bit extra." He loomed over the sweating man. "You thinking to steal from Mister Gleason?"

"Your accusations don't bother me," Willy blustered. "I'm thinking she's somewhere here, or elsewhere in town. My sister is unwell. She suffers from a weakness of the mind and I have a written evaluation stating so. Not to mention her betrothed is worried sick about her. Probably searching the premises at this very minute." With each word the man's cockiness returned. "If I were you, I'd be bringing Isadora out from wherever you've hidden her and allow her to go home with the man she's been promised to marry."

Izzy, mentally weak? *Most ridiculous thing I've ever heard.* Sam's poker face had never failed him in the past and it didn't now. "Look around, McDougall. You see any ladies? This establishment is full of gambling men. You should rejoin your game." He gestured toward Willy's empty spot, where an enterprising player edged toward the pile of abandoned chips. "Before someone else takes your place."

As Izzy's brother swore and jumped back to his slot, elbowing aside the would-be cheat, Sam slipped from the room. The urgency to ride to the Carter ranch and seek out Izzy overrode his itch to find Dalton and beat the hell out of him. This so-called *evaluation*, if there were ever such a thing, could prove a real problem, too.

Izzy needs to know.

Dalton could roam the Galleria if he wanted. Enough guards were posted around, with orders to roust and boot out anyone suspicious.

Making sure he wasn't followed, Sam exited the premises, using the kitchen door. Accustomed to seeing him come and go, Dolores merely gave a salute as he crossed the room, her attention fixed on her simmering pots.

Outside, Sam picked up speed and strode the back trail connecting businesses and the jailhouse. He'd alert Joshua to the situation before riding out to the ranch—

Rounding the Mercantile, he darted across the street and narrowly missed getting run over by a wagon and team.

"Singleton, wait up."

Squinting in the sun, Sam turned toward the familiar voice. "Elby North." He glanced over to the stocky figure sitting next to the Carter foreman. "Doc? What's going on?"

Sheaton hung on to his hat as the wagon jostled. "Missus Carter's in labor. I'm headed to the ranch."

Sam leveled a hard frown at Elby. "You came from the ranch?" As he nodded, pulling up on the team to halt their shifting, Sam demanded, "Is Miss McDougall still there?"

"She's the one who came to get me. Galloping up on that monster mustang of Harrison's. I never seen anything like it."

Sam grabbed the side bar and swung up into the wagon. "I'm coming with you."

Addie tugged on Izzy's skirts. Her lower lip trembled as she struggled with tears. "Is my mama gonna die?"

"Oh, no, darling." Izzy sank to her knees and embraced the upset child. "Doc Sheaton will help your mama as soon as he gets here, you'll see." As she spoke she winced at the sounds coming from the bedroom where Retta lay, wracked by labor misery.

She'd guided the children onto the front porch and tried to engage them in searching for ladybugs. The open windows in the house afforded some relief from the heat. Unfortunately, they also revealed Retta's distress. Izzy had done her best to distract the poor mites, but every contraction of Retta's brought on cries of her pain, which set off the siblings, until their sobs threatened to drown out their poor mama.

Izzy had no idea of how long Elby had been gone. The dedicated foreman had heard her galloping up and her breathless, "The babe's coming. Harrison needs you and your wife," was all it took for him to race for the barn, emerging a few minutes later on the broad back of a handsome palomino.

Bea, Elby's wife, had climbed up behind her husband and they'd raced for the ranch, Izzy struggling to keep pace. When he pulled on his horse's reins in front of the Carters' house, Bea leapt from the saddle and lifted her skirts to run for the house. Less than five minutes later, Elby had Harrison's team bridled to the wagon and was off toward town.

Oh, Lord, please let the doctor get here soon. She surreptitiously wiped her eyes on her sleeve.

Two-year-old Matthew crawled into Addie's lap, thumb firmly plugged between his lips. Izzy ended up holding both brother and sister since Addie wouldn't let go. Thomas, Matthew's twin, clung to Jenny who tried valiantly to settle the sturdy tot on legs not much longer than his.

In the silence broken by low cries and sobs from the open bedroom window, Bea's soothing tones, and Harrison's rumble of reassurances, Jenny rocked her brother and hummed, then warbled, "*'Sound of da rude world heard in da day, led by da moonlight've all passed away.'*"

As Izzy bent to lay her cheek on Matthew's soft hair, Addie rubbed her free arm across her nose and rasped, "*'Beautiful dreamer, queen of my song, list' while I woo thee . . .*'" A sob shook her delicate frame. "I want my mama."

"I know, sweetest one." Izzy snuggled both distraught children. Staring out past the fence, toward the widening trail, she willed Elby to return with the doctor.

Harrison's team churned up the dust as Elby jerked the reins and threw the wheel brake. Jumping off, he hurried around the snorting draft horses, dodging their pawing hooves, and helped Doc Sheaton down. The doctor dashed toward the front porch, surprisingly fast for a man in his sixties.

A childish, teary voice called, "Doc, you gonna fix my mama?"

Leaping from the back of the wagon, Sam yanked off his hat and waved away dust as a young voice screeched, "Mister Sam!" A blur of thin arms and bony knees flying off the porch was all the warning he received as Addie flung herself against him.

Holding the hand of one of the twins, Izzy followed them. Pulling away from her grasp, the boy tore down the path and snagged the back of Sam's leg.

"Hell." Sam strove to calm the children down. "It's going to be all right—oof." He staggered back as Jenny and the other twin attached themselves next. Dropping to his knees, he swept his arms around the weepy bunch. "Hush, now. Stop crying this instant."

The girls only sobbed louder and Thomas—or Matthew, it was hard to say which one—started hiccupping.

Finally, Addie drew away and stared at first Sam, then Izzy. "You won't let bad things happen to my mama, will you?" Her lower lip trembled.

"Between Doc Sheaton and your daddy, nothing bad will happen," Izzy promised. "Missus Bea is helping, too."

She glanced at Sam with such hope, he could only nod and pray she was right.

Chapter 9

Harrison's brother and his wife Catherine had arrived twenty minutes earlier. Catherine had immediately disappeared into Retta's bedroom while Frank set up a frantic pace between the front parlor and the kitchen. The few times Izzy had met Frank Carter, he'd intimidated her with his bear-like appearance and gruff demeanor, reminding her disturbingly of her brother Willy. It surely wasn't a fair comparison, since he'd always treated her kindly.

Every time Frank came near, she tensed. As if recognizing his effect on her, he made a point of keeping his distance, which only made her feel even more like a coward. Izzy hated the fact she'd allowed herself to become so meek and timid since Mama's disappearance.

Seeking comfort, Jenny had crawled onto Izzy's lap an hour earlier. Looking for comfort herself, she held the child tight and added her own silent prayers for Retta and her newborn's safety. Addie sat near the fireplace, wringing her hands as she stared into the flames. Izzy grimaced. No six-year-old should ever have to experience such a level of despair.

Samuel had been on the floor trying to keep the twins busy, allowing them to climb all over him, clutching him with chubby, anxious fists. Izzy found herself touched by the gentle way the hardened gambler had with two clinging tots, tickling bellies and pretending to fall into fits when they gouged his sides and beneath his arms in reciprocation.

The man continued to surprise her.

Finally, the sound of a babe's cry sent a rush of relief through her, and she instinctively sought out Samuel to share her joy. He returned her gaze with matching gladness, sweeping Thomas and Matthew into a hug.

Izzy had discovered more about Samuel's character today. She'd already learned he was a good, honorable, and decent man, now she knew he also had a solid core of strength and kindness. It warmed her, the way he'd spent the last couple hours entertaining the children, doing his best to draw their attention away from Retta's cries and Harrison's prayers.

Doc Sheaton entered the room, wiping his stained hands on a towel. Izzy smothered a gasp at the sight of blood, hoping Addie and the other children hadn't seen it. While Samuel continued to distract the boys, Izzy shielded their sisters' view of the doctor as he made for the kitchen and the wash basin in the sink.

Figuring Bea had remained in the room with Catherine, Izzy waited for news of the birth and Retta's health.

No such reaction from Frank, however, who strode across the room with keen focus, nearly throbbing with tension as he loomed in the doorway. "Dammit, Doc, how's Retta and the babe?"

The doctor returned to the front room, drying off on a clean towel, and tossed Frank a warning look. Plastering on a sedate smile, his gaze encompassed the children. "Your mama is going to be fine, and you have a new little sister."

Something in his tone set Izzy on edge, and she nervously chewed on her lower lip.

Frank offered his nieces and nephews a smile of reassurance. "Shortcake, how about you take your brothers and sister outside so your mama can have some quiet time."

Eyes red from crying, Addie wiped her nose on her sleeve. "All right, Uncle Frank." She motioned to her siblings. "Come on, Mama needs to rest." She scooped up one of the twins, while Jenny hopped off Izzy's lap and grabbed the hand of the other. "We'll play on the swing."

Once the children were outside, Frank's smile faded as he barked out, "What aren't you telling us?"

Doc Sheaton gestured impatiently. "Keep your voice down, Frank. Missus Carter is going to be fine. You'll need to ask her anything else."

Catherine entered from the hallway, coming up next to her husband. "Shush, now. Retta's resting and Harrison's holding her and our new niece." She exhaled sadly. "Retta asked me to share the news with everyone, since she knows you are all worrying."

Frank's gruff demeanor evaporated like steam escaping a boiling kettle. One large palm tenderly cupped Catherine's cheek. "What is it, darlin'?"

The clear adoration in his voice sent a pang of envy through Izzy. What would it be like to have a man love her that way? Once again, her gaze slid to Samuel whose eyes were locked on her instead of the drama playing out in front of them. She quickly lowered her lashes.

Catherine stated, "It appears Retta won't be able to conceive any more children." When her husband paled, she hastened to add, "They're taking it well, Frank."

"Damn," Frank muttered, staring down Doc Sheaton. "Are you certain?"

The doctor's bushy white brows drew together. "We can't know for sure, son. From my years of practice, after a rough birth like Retta endured, the likelihood of her bearing another child is slim. And dangerous. For her health and safety, it's better this way."

Catherine clasped Frank's arm. "We need to prepare the buckboard so we can take Retta back to town."

"Why to town?"

"Maisy'll take good care of her," Doc Sheaton replied. He headed for the hallway. "I'll get my bag while you help Harrison gather some things for Retta."

Focused on what the doctor had to say, Izzy jumped when Samuel suddenly stood next to her. She hadn't even seen him move.

"Maisy's the Doc's wife," he said quietly. "The woman's also a renowned midwife. She'll be able to see that Retta gets the care she needs."

"Ah, I see," Izzy murmured as Frank and Catherine left to prepare for the trip back to town. She met Samuel's solemn stare. They hadn't had a chance to speak yet, so she still didn't know why he'd come out to the ranch with Doc Sheaton.

As if reading her mind, he muttered, "We need to talk." He guided her into the kitchen and over to the table, settling her in one chair while he took another.

The intensity of his stare made her pulse race, and not in a good way. "Is something wrong?"

"I'm afraid so." Samuel cupped her face, setting off those tingles inside her again. "Your brother came back to town today." He frowned at her gasp of fright. "I won't let him hurt you, Izzy."

"How can we stop him from taking me away?" She didn't think she'd have the strength to withstand Willy or her father's demands. They'd physically force her and suffer no guilt. Though women had made some advances in their rights over the past decade, arranged marriages were still far too common.

Samuel shifted in his seat. "I've put a lot of thought into that and can only think of one way to protect you." Though his lips curved in a smile, his eyes remained dark and deep.

Her brows furrowed. "What is it?"

His gaze softened. "Izzy McDougall, will you do me the honor of becoming my wife?"

Sam pulled Harrison's buggy to a stop alongside the larger buckboard carrying Retta and Doc Sheaton. Unwilling to leave the children in one of the miner wives' care, Harrison had piled them in next to their mother. For once the little heathens behaved themselves, sitting quietly around Retta as she lay on cushioning blankets, holding the new babe. Bea North's offer to launder and clean up from the birth afforded both Retta and Harrison some relief.

Frank and Catherine had ridden in on their matched pair, a black-as-night stud and a dainty mare, both chomping at the bit, eager to run. An expert equestrian, Catherine handled her mare with ease, and Frank's stallion certainly understood who his master was.

Climbing down from the buggy, he helped a visibly anxious Izzy to the ground. It'd taken him the entire return trip to convince her the best option to stop her family from forcing her into a union with Reginald Dalton was to marry him instead. Sam had shared her brother's exact words concerning this supposed evaluation regarding her mental incapacity, watching as she'd puffed up in anger, then deflated when she understood how far her family would go to control her.

The McDougall men conspired with Dalton in the most heinous way, a final last bit of information that convinced her.

"Are you sure about this, Mister Singleton?" she asked. "Why would you tie yourself to a woman you don't love?"

The way she insisted on calling him by his surname both amused and exasperated him. "I'm sure."

He'd posed that same question to himself at least a dozen times, coming up with the same answer. He couldn't allow her, so beautiful and kind, to be hurt. After only a short span of time, he cared for her a great deal. Any man would be lucky to have her as his wife, and Sam was her best chance to escape a bleak life with a cruel man.

He'd spent years skirting the edges of the law, first in a bid to survive, then as a way to better his chances. Maybe because of his past mistakes, he didn't deserve a fine, outstanding woman like Izzy McDougall.

Won't stop me from claiming her.

Marriages had started out on shakier foundations and succeeded. Both Carter brothers were prime examples. Sam had heard the stories from Hannah Gleason, herself an admitted romantic. She'd sighed over Harrison's decision to marry Retta despite expecting her older sister who'd been terminally ill and unable to join him in Little Creede. Frank's marriage to Catherine, also begun for the wrong reasons, resulted in an enduring passion considered unusual and rare by current standards.

Surely he'd find himself fortunate enough to make a similar match.

Attempting to put his bride-to-be at ease, Sam opted for teasing her. "Since we're soon to be wed, shouldn't you call me Sam?"

She shifted nervously. "I-I don't know." She redirected her attention to where Harrison cradled his wife and babe in his arms, following Doc Sheaton toward his office.

So shy, Sam thought. And so young. Yet there was much more to Izzy than even she would understand. Modest and unassuming she might be, yet Sam had also spotted a core of steel within her slight frame. Strength she'd needed to survive the cruelty served up by the men in her family. The woman had already lived a lifetime of sorrow in her scant years on this earth.

Not any longer, he promised himself.

Aware of several townsfolk gathered here and there, not so subtle in their open staring, Sam waited for Frank and Catherine to join them, each holding one of the twins, while Addie followed with Jenny, a firm grip on her sister's arm.

"Are you really gettin' married, Mister Sam?" Addie jumped up and down in excitement. "Can I come? Please?"

Next to her Jenny clapped her hands. "I wanna see a married, too." She blinked up at Addie. "What's a married?"

"It's like what Mama an' Papa do. They're married," Addie explained patiently.

"Oh." Jenny blinked up at Sam. "Den you gets a sister like us?"

"Lordy," Izzy groaned under her breath.

Sam itched to respond, but Frank spoiled the moment by nudging his nieces toward Catherine who made no secret of her amusement as she balanced a twin on her hip and motioned to the girls.

"Come, you two troublemakers," she admonished. "We're going to see Reverend Matias."

"I'm not a troublemaker," Addie protested, dragging her feet. "An' it's not Sunday."

"*Now,* Adeline Marie Carter."

As they trod after their aunt, Frank came beside Sam, jiggling his nephew to keep him quiet. "So, you're really doing this?"

Longing to wipe off the man's annoying smirk, Sam didn't bother responding. Instead, he grasped Izzy's elbow and steered her down the boardwalk toward the church at the opposite end of town.

Pausing only briefly to straighten her skirts, she came along.

"We're gettin' a married," Jenny screeched to anyone within hearing distance, fairly vibrating with excitement.

"Wedding," Addie corrected, rolling her eyes as she tried to rein in the bouncing toddler.

The townsfolk began to follow them, bits and pieces of discussion echoing in their wake, from open speculation to enthusiasm over how it'd been too long since anyone had gotten hitched in Little Creede.

Ben Parsons met them halfway to the church, one quizzical brow arched as he called out, "Are you really marryin' today, Sam?"

Sam nodded curtly, maintaining an urgent pace. If he slowed down, the woman at his side could change her mind. In his gut, he knew she was in grave danger, and the only way to keep her from harm was if he legally had the right to protect her. He had to admit, going about it this way probably wasn't his smartest move.

"Well, I better go get Trudy," Ben shouted after them. "She'll make me sleep in the barn for a month if I allow her to miss a wedding."

Sam felt like a mother duck, herding hatchlings. A long line of people straggled out behind them, all chattering about upcoming nuptials. He spotted Hannah, sitting beside the widely grinning Knight Gleason in his fancy curricle, the stallion's tight reins slowing his steps around potholes as he shook his thick mane and snorted. How the hell had the news reached the Galleria so fast?

Vivian Lang skipped across the street to the side of the rig, holding up her skirts and grinning, keeping easy pace. "Where's Maggie?" she hollered.

Hannah's response floated away on the warm breeze. Sam figured Maggie and Robert had to be somewhere in the circus-like melee. Doggedly, he pushed forward with his plans and his soon-to-be wife.

As they passed the Adams Boardinghouse, Maude Adams hollered, "Nice day for a weddin', ain't it?" Next to the elderly widow's rocking chair, Hank Soames, the aged gent who'd been courting her off and on the past few months, stood and whistled out both sides of his mostly toothless mouth.

"Nosy old gal," Sam grumbled under his breath, fighting back the urge to laugh. Little Creede's oldest resident had surely earned the right to be a busybody. He raised his free arm and waved.

By the time they reached the church, Reverend Matias was standing at the door, wearing an amused expression. "Well, what have we here?"

Sam wasted no time. "Can you marry us today, Matias?"

The Reverend's nearly black eyes locked on Izzy. "Is that what you want, young lady?"

"I-I—"

At her hesitancy, Sam raised her hand to his lips and kissed her knuckles. "From this day forward, Izzy, your happiness and welfare will be my greatest responsibility. Please marry me."

"Oh, how romantic," someone sighed from the crowd, while others began taking bets on her answer, with a few calling out encouragements for her to accept.

He knew the minute she'd made her decision as she pulled her shoulders back, determination entering her gaze. "Yes, Mister Samuel, I'll marry you."

Sam offered her a nod of approval as they followed the Reverend inside. Unable to resist a final tease, he murmured, "Sam, honey. Just Sam."

Chapter 10

Once Samuel guided Izzy into Reverend Matias's church and toward the altar, her panic started up again, a thousand buzzing bees under her skin. Though she didn't exactly dig in her heels, each slowing step she managed past the tiny church nave felt strangling to her.

Of course she'd dreamt of her wedding; what young girl hadn't? Hers centered around a pretty gown, perhaps flowers in her hair and a nosegay she'd carry down the aisle on her way to the man of her dreams. Mama would have cried happy tears into one of her dainty embroidered handkerchiefs . . .

She'd learned dreams were not for everyone, most of her hopes dashed when Mama went missing and Papa and Willy started plotting.

Low murmurs broke into her dark thoughts. Izzy realized she'd stopped abruptly, halfway to the altar. Beside her, Samuel paused as well, and to his credit didn't tug on her or try to urge her further. He brought her around and stared into her face which suddenly felt hotter than banked coals on a cookstove.

She raised her eyes to his, expecting anger and irritation.

He bent to her ear and whispered, "What is it, honey? What can I do to make this better for you?"

"I want—" She swallowed, an audible click against her tongue. How could she explain without sounding ungrateful for everything Samuel and Little Creede's townsfolk had done for her?

Never losing eye contact with her, Samuel waited, until she managed, "My gown is all dusty, and I know I have dirt on my face." She bit her tongue, refusing to say any more lest he think worse of her.

"Is that all? Nothing we can't fix, sweet Izzy."

Samuel motioned someone over and suddenly Vivian stood beside her. "Let me see." In front of everyone she took hold of Izzy's chin. "Why, all I see is an itty-bitty spot, right here." She fumbled in her pocket and drew out a square of linen as delicate as anything Mama might have carried.

Vivian dabbed a corner of the soft cloth to Izzy's left cheek. "There, now, all gone. Anything else?"

Izzy cleared her throat. "My skirt. Grass stains."

"Hmm." Vivian made a half-circle around her, declaring, "Not one speck of grass, truly. What else?"

As Izzy scrambled for more reasons why this was a bad idea, Addie and Jenny came thundering down the aisle, each holding a fistful of hastily picked flowers. Jenny's offering boasted clumps of earth stuck to its roots.

"Here." Addie thrust hers at Izzy. "You gotta have flowers to get married."

"Me, too," Jenny urged, holding her limp posies out. "For married."

Slowly Izzy gathered the drooping flowers into a nosegay. "It's the prettiest thing I ever saw," she vowed, emotion threatening to choke her.

While several women in the church exclaimed softly, and a few men harrumphed as if to hide their own reactions, Izzy turned toward her bridegroom, whose wide grin broke over her like sunlight.

"I'm ready."

To Sam's everlasting relief, Matias kept the ceremony short.

Shoulder to shoulder with his skittish bride, standing at the altar took on a kind of surreal quality, someplace he had never imagined he'd be. Growing up hard and fast, Sam had no experience with family. What he'd discovered along the way could be whittled down to his first year in Little Creede, observing how the Carters acted around each other. Never had he imagined becoming a family man himself, not after the sort of hardscrabble life he'd endured—

"Do you have a ring?"

Matias's low query broke into the churn of his mind, and Sam blinked, meeting the reverend's somewhat amused eyes. "What?"

"A ring, son, for your bride. A symbol of your devotion."

"I—" Sam caught himself before he cursed aloud in church. Glancing to the side, noting Izzy's flaming red cheeks, he clamped down on his wayward tongue. Why the hell would he carry a ring around in his pocket? He blotted at the perspiration on his forehead, the glint of his signet catching his attention.

Slowly he pulled it from his little finger, a token he'd won during his poker days on Gleason's Mississippi riverboat. It came off easily, and he held it up. "Will this do for now?"

"I do believe it will. Place the ring on her finger, Sam," Matias intoned solemnly. Though his expression remained placid, Sam swore the man held back a chuckle.

Two seconds later the ring, small as it was, spun on Izzy's slender digit. She raised widened eyes to his, their pretty blue-gray darkened with an emotion he couldn't define. "I'll get you a better one that fits," Sam whispered.

She blushed adorably. "I like this one."

The moment seemed to stretch out for an eternity, the subtle chatter from the pews fading into nothing. Sam's heartbeat kicked up and the pink in Izzy's cheeks deepened to match the wilted flowers she still clutched. Dimly, he heard Matias pronounce them married. The edges of his brain registered the words, "Kiss your bride."

He wanted to kiss her, right on those soft, full lips. He started to lean in, then saw how they trembled. Young, untried, scared. Vulnerable. If he kissed her now, would he taste fear?

Sam brought her left hand up to his lips and kissed her knuckles, lingering over the silky skin. Izzy's sharp intake of breath made him yearn for more—much more—from her. Her eyes sparkled with happiness, her mouth no longer trembling. He'd made the right choice.

Tucking her against his side, he guided her down the aisle amidst a grin here and a sigh there from the folks assembled. A few men saluted him approvingly, too. As he and Izzy passed Gleason and his missus, the flamboyant gambler winked broadly.

Outside, the sun shone its heat and brightness on the path leading back to the center of town. Sam led his new wife over to the old cottonwood tree with its thick-branched leaves and abundant shade. Her smile never dimming, she leaned against the rough trunk.

He peered down at her. "Howdy-do, Missus Singleton."

"Hello, Mister Singleton." She raised the sorry nosegay in her grip. "I don't think these can be saved."

"No, they're done for. Jenny will pick you more. You don't even have to ask." Both Carter girls tore out the front door of the church, headed right for them. "Brace yourself."

"What? Hey!" She grunted as they flung themselves against her, almost dragging her to her knees. "Well, look what I caught." Slinging an arm around each, she squeezed them. "Thank you for my flowers."

Addie frowned at what was left of the wilted things. "We can get you more."

"No, that's not necessary—"

"More fowers! C'mon, sissy." Jenny tugged on Addie until she released Izzy. The girls darted toward a side yard to a patch of flowers they had no doubt already raided.

"Oh, dear. Will the Reverend be angry?" As Izzy made to follow them, Sam grabbed for her arm. She turned to him, frowning. "I don't want to see them get into trouble."

"They'll be fine. The Reverend's missus plants a patch for the young'uns to enjoy."

"Oh. Such a thoughtful thing to do." When the remainder of their wedding attendees poured out of the gaping doors of the church, she went as still as a startled doe.

Vivian met them first, sweeping Izzy into a warm hug, while Frank and then Harrison slapped Sam on the back. Over their well-wishes, he heard Vivian proclaim, "Now you'll be safe, Izzy."

Sam made a silent vow her statement would forever ring true.

Catherine hugged Izzy next. Pivoting to Sam, she raised on tiptoe to plant a kiss on his cheek. "We can rustle up some refreshments back at the Stage House. Newly wedded folks need a bit of fussing-over."

"Stop kissing him," Frank growled, though he tempered it with a smirk and a wink.

She cuddled into her husband's side. "Bossy man."

"I'm headed over to Doc's," Harrison said, dropping his hat back on his head. "I'm sure everything's fine with Retta and the babe, but I'll be staying there until further notice."

"Got a name for that scrap of a girl, yet?" Sam asked, more to entertain Izzy and include her in town familiarity than out of curiosity.

Harrison beamed. "Retta chose Quinn. It was her mama's maiden name." He regarded his brother. "You want to take the brood over to Ma's for me?"

"Sure. She's got Charity. And Isiah's already there, getting spoiled rotten. The boys are still in the nave, probably playing hide-a-seek under Matias's robes." Frank started toward the door, Catherine trailing behind. "We'll bring them to Doc's first so they can see their new sister."

One by one, the remaining townsfolk offered congratulations, a few suggestions for the wedding night, and other comments made in good cheer. Edging Izzy toward the church path and away from the well-meaning bunch, Sam endured more back-slapping from those he knew and a few others he vaguely recalled being involved with the tourney. Which had ended early this morning, so why hadn't all these fools gone home?

Knight and Hannah soon joined the celebration, Hannah clinging to his arm. "Well now, Mistuh an' Missus Singleton. Ah'm right happy fer yew both." He pressed his whiskered cheek to Izzy's, while Hannah embraced her from the other side. Knight straightened and shook Sam's hand vigorously. "Now, yew an' yer lil' bride'll need a proper weddin' night. An' ah got just what yew need."

"I helped redecorate," Hannah put in, all smiles. "You know which room, Sam." At his raised brows, she giggled. "You're a married man now. No more 'Mister Samuel' for you."

"All right," he agreed, charmed anew by Knight's tenderhearted wife.

Sobering, he recalled what room his employer spoke of, an expansive suite fitted out like the worst riverboat bordello. "I appreciate the offer, but—"

"None of that." Knight's cuff on Sam's shoulder about laid him flat. "It's our gift an' yew'd be makin' me an' mah lil' dove heah happy if'n yew accept."

"Well, I—"

He broke off at Izzy's sharp gasp and stared down at her. She'd gone chalk-white. "Izzy?"

"Oh, no." The words trembled on her lips, a mere thread as she stared past him. "My . . ."

Sam spun, reaching for his holster at the sight of Willy McDougall strutting up the street as if he owned every speck of dirt under his boots. Beside him, dandified like something out of a fancy drawing room, a tall, wide-shouldered and barrel-chested older man kept pace. *Reginald Dalton, I'd wager.* Trailing both of them was a plump, white-haired man who could only be Izzy's father, the resemblance to his son strong even from a distance.

Pivoting slowly, Sam examined the lingering crowd, mostly women and a few children. "Dammit," he muttered.

Frank was inside the church, rounding up his unruly nephews; Harrison at Sheaton's office. Ben had already left, escorting his wife back to the Stage House. After the ceremony, Sam had briefly spotted Robert and Maggie, strolling up the street to somewhere, perhaps the Galleria. He hadn't seen Joshua, not surprising since the sheriff wouldn't have left the jail unattended.

Beside him, Knight stiffened, unobtrusively tucking Hannah behind him, the same as Sam had done with Izzy. "What the hell is that idjit still a-doin' heah?"

"Izzy," Sam said softly. "Take Hannah and go into the church. Send Frank out." He hugged her reassuringly. "If there's any other men in there, tell them to come out, too."

She clung to his arm. "I don't want to leave you."

"Yew go on now, with mah wife, Missus Izzy. Take care of her fer me, kin yew do that?" Knight gave Hannah a light push toward Izzy, and Sam sighed in relief when the two women clutched each other and hurried into the church.

"Now what?" Knight's big paws dropped to his holster. "Yer call, Sam."

"We wait."

They didn't have to wait long. Both McDougall men and Dalton sped up, striding faster, until they reached the beginning of the path leading to the church grounds.

Out of the corner of his eye, Sam saw women scattering, taking children with them. He counted two men remaining, one of them Jaworski, the smithy whose casual stance belied his alertness.

Willy surged forward. "Where the hell is my sister, Singleton?" Beside him, Dalton stood, feet planted apart, toying with his pistol handles, as the elder William shuffled his feet.

Sam thumbed up the brim of his slouch. "No idea what you're talking about, McDougall."

"I saw her. Standing next to you with some fat cow."

"Ah'm gonna kill 'em," Knight growled, bristling worse than a charging grizzly.

"Easy, boss." Sam edged the enraged gambler aside. "You don't want to end up in Territorial with a child on the way."

Knight subsided, snarling low in his throat, as Sam remained loose-hipped and relaxed. It wouldn't take much to provoke Izzy's brother into drawing and shooting. Of the three confronting him, it was obvious Junior was the most unstable.

"Poker tourney's over, McDougall. Unless you stayed around to help clean up, you should be on your way now."

With grim amusement he'd recognized the shiny revolvers in Dalton's tooled holster. Remingtons were no match for the powerful Peacemakers Sam had won in a game of five-card stud, back in '78. He figured the man was also too dumb to realize he'd be dead on the ground if he dared draw.

"We ain't leaving without Isadora," Willy shouted, growing more agitated. He gestured to his companion. "Mister Dalton here is her betrothed, come to collect what's his." He advanced another foot or so up the path. Izzy's father hadn't moved at all other than to study the ground as if fascinated by dirt.

Dalton joined Willy, pistols hanging low on his hips, picking up glints from the sun.

"Yew want me to shoot him?" Knight muttered, shifting impatiently. "Ah'll take 'em out fer sport." He eyed the older man with disdain. "That theah suit coat needs to be put outta its misery."

"Stay ready," Sam replied, determined not to give in to his employer, though Knight could be damned amusing. Now wasn't the time.

Behind him vague murmurs came and went, the clink of spurs as men shifted in place, the shush of a window opening as if seeking a breeze. Sam didn't have to turn to acknowledge a cocked rifle now pointed out toward the threesome.

A single rustle of grass next to him and a low, "Matias has them in sight," was all the assurance Sam needed as Frank stepped up next to him. "What d'ya wanna do?"

"We let them leave, unharmed. We've got nothing firm on them yet, except for being stupider than mud," Sam retorted softly. He raised his voice, turning slightly to meet Dalton head-on. "Mister, you have no claim over my wife. I think it's time for you and my new family-by-marriage to take yourselves back to Silver Cache."

All three men's reaction to 'wife' was enough for Frank and Knight to visibly stiffen.

Willy tugged his pistol—a womanly-looking .22 Short, for Christ's sake—from its holster. "You're a lying bastard! Isadora wouldn't shirk her duty. She's been promised to another since she was sixteen."

"Put away your gun, you hothead. It solves nothing, and we all need to remain civilized," Dalton commented, his rasp at odds with the fancy slicked-back hair and cuffed, striped trousers. He dusted off his coat sleeve, appearing unruffled by the potential violence surrounding him.

Willy groused, re-holstering his weapon.

Dalton's deep-set eyes gave him a stony appearance even from yards away, as he addressed Sam directly. "I have an agreement with William McDougall the Third." He waved toward Izzy's portly father. "As well as his blessing to wed Miss Isadora McDougall by her twentieth birthday." He rolled his shoulders as if bored. "Miss Isadora is mine."

"You hear that, Singleton?" Willy took a wider stance and rested visibly trigger-happy fingers on his holster. "Bring her out, now."

Frank swung abreast of Sam, poised and threatening to behold. Willy's eyes widened but he didn't back down, proving himself impulsive and plumb crazy not to retreat when confronted by a Carter. Sam remained immobile as well, knowing any sudden moves could cost innocent lives should this trio of pestilence start shooting.

Praying the women wouldn't burst through the church doors, Sam casually hooked his thumbs in his holster, a ruse he'd learned as a young hired gun. In this position his draw was even faster. "You gents aren't in any trouble. Yet. If you turn around and leave, peacefully, you'll remain that way. There's nothing for any of you in this town."

"You got no legal right," Willy snarled. "I'm from a long line of lawyers, I oughta know. Mister Dalton signed a writ of marriage agreement."

"Yes, I did." Dalton caressed the tops of his inferior revolvers while Sam kept a steady focus on his antics. One wrong move and the man would die where he stood. "Verified in a court of law in Silver Cache," he continued genially. "We thought it prudent to have the judge there as a witness." The cold gleam in his eyes belied the excessively polite tone.

"What a load of horseshit," Frank muttered. "I'd lay money there's no such thing. Judge Wilson is as straight as the day is long."

Sam didn't know the judge personally but Frank vouching for his honesty was good enough. "Forgive me if I call you on your stinking lie—"

A flash of bright blue gingham and dark, bouncing braids interrupted, along with a high, excited, "I got fowers, Mista Sam!"

Sam froze. Frank groaned, "Ah, hell," as Jenny Carter skipped across the lawn and right into the path of overwhelming danger.

Chapter 11

Sam's gut knotted with panic for the darling little girl standing in the middle of a showdown, a bundle of daisies clutched in her tiny hands. The stench of barely restrained violence hung in the air, worse than cow flop on a blistering hot day.

Proudly showing off her bouquet, Jenny held them up to Willy. "See what I pick'd." A giggle floated in the air.

Willy's calculating gaze fell to the child, and he made a sudden grab for her.

The cocking of a rifle echoed alongside a growling, "Don't touch her."

Willy spun around and cursed.

Joshua Lang held his Winchester repeater against the back of Dalton's head. A single bullet from its powerful cartridge would blow his skull all over the church path if Lang pulled the trigger. A weapon favored by Texas Rangers, the sheriff had wisely kept his long after he'd quit the organization.

Frank rushed in and swept Jenny up, carrying her away from danger. Addie stood nearby, mouth agape, panting from chasing after her sister. He handed Jenny off to her, ordering briskly, "Take her inside, Shortcake."

Seconds seemed to drag into an eternity until Addie rushed Jenny toward the church.

Dalton's jaw clenched as the rifle muzzle prodded the back of his head. "There's no need for violence," he grated out. "We aren't here to cause trouble, only to retrieve my betrothed—"

"Shut your mouth." The thought that this pompous dandy believed his money could buy someone as precious as Izzy for his filthy pleasures, filled Sam with a murderous rage. "My wife belongs to no man but me." His fingers flexed hard above his holstered Colts with the urge to pump double rounds into the man's worthless heart. "I'll kill anyone who tries to take her."

A brusque throat-clearing brought everyone's attention to the elder William, who'd up to this point stood silently by. "Mister Singleton, the wedding isn't legal." He paused, indicating his coat lapel. "If I may?"

Sam immediately pulled his gun. Around him, the whisper of weapons being drawn echoed in the hot air as the rest of the menfolk pointed pistols at the elder McDougall. All except Joshua, who had eased his rifle from Dalton's head and now held it steady at chest-level. Frank aimed at Willy, the motley trio of intruders surrounded.

McDougall froze. "I'm only going for a document. Don't shoot." With exaggerated slowness, the man retrieved a folded piece of paper from an inner vest pocket. "Mister Dalton spoke correctly. I have here a contract, signed by my daughter and later filed by the court at Silver Cache once we became residents there."

Sam flinched when Izzy protested, "I signed no such thing."

She hurried to his side. He'd have rather kept her out of this, but since she was already here, he brought his arm around her slender waist. The feel of her soft curves against him held a magnitude of rightness. The need to protect her settled deep into his soul.

Leaning into him, she fisted his shirt. "I would never agree to nor sign anything like that."

The panic in her voice ramped up his fury. Sam ignored the paper her father held out. "My wife says you're mistaken, Mister McDougall."

"Gentlemen, my daughter is emotionally unstable. Why, I have additional documentation from a physician who treated her for a predisposition to female hysteria. Reginald was kind enough to offer for her hand in marriage, where she'll get the best medical treatment money can buy. Isadora agreed to this arrangement, and it's too late for her to back out now."

Sam had heard enough. "I suggest you all get back into your fancy wagon over there"—he nodded toward the lavish buggy visible near the edge of the Stage House property line—"and ride out of Little Creede. Don't come back."

Willy blustered, "You ain't the law, Singleton."

Joshua advanced until all three men could see the badge pinned to his vest, identifying him as a lawman. "But *I* am. Now, you heard the man." He flicked the muzzle of his rifle toward the center of town. "Git, before I decide you're a threat and lock your hides in jail."

"You can't arrest us," Willy screeched, while his father and Dalton bristled.

The smile that spread across Joshua's face wasn't warm and friendly. "I can, and I will. Your choice."

Willy opened his mouth, ready to spew more bullshit. His father clamped a hand on his shoulder, silencing him. "Enough, son." His cold gaze flicked to Izzy.

Sam shifted, shielding her from her father's aggressiveness. "My wife is no longer your concern. You have something to say, you say it to me."

"Fine." McDougall settled a calculating glare on Sam as he brandished the paper in his grip. "This is a binding contract signed and notarized in front of a prominent judge back East, and it's legally enforceable here in Colorado. That said, my daughter is more Mister Dalton's than yours."

"I didn't sign it." Izzy clutched the back of Sam's shirt. Her voice cracked. "He's lying."

"Sheriff." Sam caught Joshua's attention. "Would I be within my rights to shoot a man who tried to harm my wife?"

Lang's hard glare never wavered, nor did his rifle. "I reckon so, Sam."

"Good to know." Sam fired into the dirt in front of the men, spitting up gravel. Willy stumbled back into his father, who roughly shoved him away.

"You'll be sorry," the elder McDougall threatened, stomping across the grass toward the path leading to the Stage House. Wordlessly, Reginald Dalton followed, both climbing in the buggy, Dalton taking up the reins.

Willy stood there, knuckles bunched at his sides. "You can't get away with this. Isadora belongs to us."

Not bothering to answer, Sam hauled off with another round, nearly hitting the man in the foot. Muttering threats, Willy spun and dashed into the street, waving his arms to make the buggy stop as Dalton snapped the reins and the horses began to clop away. Taking a running leap, Willy dove for the footstep and scrambled on.

Izzy stood in the doorway of the Galleria suite Hannah Gleason had offered them and gaped at its opulence. Never had she seen anything so fine, not even in Chicago.

Against a backdrop of dark green wallpaper brocaded with fleur-de-lis, golden oak paneling surrounded a fireplace with a marbled mantel. Cabbage rose carpets covered the floor, small occasional tables held ornately etched hurricane lamps with neatly trimmed wicks, and a matched pair of oak rockers sat in front of the hearth. Soft muslin panels fluttered in the breeze from three open windows.

Her gaze landed on the bed, positioned in the center of the suite. Overhead, hand-tatted lace formed a canopy, held in place by carved oak posts. Someone had taken great care with the coverlet, warm ivory like the window panels and trimmed in flowering bands of deep rose and verdant green. Pillows echoed the colors, piled against the headboard. The mattress was so high off the floor, a wooden stepstool had been set to the side in order to assist in breaching it. The only other pieces of furniture in the suite consisted of a lovely highboy and a washstand containing everything needed for morning ablutions.

Hannah had already explained they would find a copper tub behind the latticework screen placed at the opposite end of the room, should they desire a bath.

The entire effect rendered Izzy speechless and panicky.

Without any other furniture for seating, save the rocking chairs, it'd become apparent the only sleeping area was the elegantly appointed bed.

The thought of sharing a bed with Samuel both excited and frightened her.

"Sam," she corrected in a whisper too low for him to hear. She needed to remember it was what he preferred to be called.

A tremble rolled up her spine. Her legs shook, her vision dimming, as her blood thrummed in her veins. Her throat suddenly felt tight. As a child, she'd been sheltered. Then, after her mother's disappearance she'd been a prisoner with no womanly influence to prepare her for married life. What would her husband require of her on their wedding night?

He crossed the room to her. "Izzy, nothing's happening in bed tonight except sleep." He slid a fingertip along the curve of her ear. "I need to step out for a bit to discuss tomorrow's faro game with

Knight. Hannah left a nightshift for you. Why don't you change and crawl into bed?"

Some of her tension eased. She needed time to herself so she could gather her thoughts and courage. Her head spun from the changes this day had wrought in her life. "All right," she said.

"I won't be long."

After he left, her pulse slowed to normal and she took her first full breath since entering the room.

"My goodness." Amazement swept over her. *I'm a married woman now.*

Never in her life would she have thought her husband would be anyone as good and decent as Samuel Singleton. Growing into adulthood, she'd recognized her father would put his business dealings above her wellbeing and figured she'd someday wed a man she didn't love. She had hoped the man would at least be kind, her worst nightmare the fear of ending up with a husband as cruel as Reginald Dalton.

"Missus Singleton," she whispered into the room, liking the way it sounded when spoken aloud.

A sense of comfort began to repair her broken spirit. Already she knew she could trust her new husband to keep her safe. Remembering the women of Little Creede embracing her as one of their own, and how their men had come to her defense, brought tears of gratitude to her eyes.

I think I finally found a home.

Realizing she'd been standing there like a ninny, daydreaming, she dug inside the highboy for the promised nightshift, finding a demure garment of white smocked batiste that would cover her as well as any of her gowns.

She offered Hannah silent thanks. Unsure if she was prepared for the intimacies of marriage, Izzy found herself grateful to Sam as well, for not rushing her.

Disrobing, she hung her gown, chemise, and corset on a wooden peg next to the washstand, then poured a generous amount of water from the pitcher into the ceramic bowl for a quick sponge bath. Not finding a brush, the best she could do was to finger-comb her curls. The cool air sent a shiver over her damp skin, and she retrieved the nightshift, easing it over her head.

The sun, lowering in the horizon, painted soft shadows across the suite. Izzy turned when the door opened and Sam entered. His gaze encompassed her in one glance as he set the latch. "You look especially lovely tonight, Missus Singleton."

Feeling daring, Izzy batted her lashes in the flirtatious manner she'd seen Catherine Carter use on her husband, hoping she didn't look foolish. "Thank you, Mister Singleton."

His low laughter stirred up butterflies in her stomach as he crossed the room to where she stood. "Ready for bed, Wife?"

Izzy's calm scattered, and she bit her bottom lip. "Y-Yes," she lied.

His steady gaze held her captive. "What did I say earlier?"

"That we would just, er, sleep."

"I meant it, too. I'd never do anything that'd hurt you or make you regret our marriage. As your husband, it's up to me to see to your happiness and comfort. I take those responsibilities seriously."

He removed his vest and holster. While Izzy stood transfixed, he shrugged out of his shirt and hung it next to her gown. Teasing eyes locked on her, he unbuckled his belt and slipped it out of the loops. "I sleep in my drawers, honey. Your virtue is safe."

When he loosened his suspenders and unfastened the first button of his trousers, Izzy spun to the bed and tugged back the coverlet, lifting her gown so she could use the stepstool.

"What the hell?" Samuel barked out.

Startled, she swung back around and found a very angry man glaring at her. Betrayal and fear crashed into her.

Sam's eyes held the same anger as her father's when he'd beat her.

With an agonized moan of denial, Izzy raced for the door. Sam got there first and slapped both hands on the jamb, trapping her. Heat from his body poured off him, chasing away the last of her chills. His harsh breathing puffed against her ear.

Fear clogged her throat as her emotions churned. Why was he so angry? She pressed her forehead against the door and squeezed her eyes shut, her husband's woodsy scent surrounding her.

"Izzy, look at me." He clasped her shoulders and turned her around. "I didn't mean to scare you. And I swear, I'd never hurt you."

Unwilling to witness the man she'd learned to trust strike the first blow, she couldn't comply. Not until his choked-out plea of, "Please, Izzy," did she open her eyes. His naked chest filled her vision. She tried not to react as her breathing sped up.

When she finally looked up, apology shone in his tender gaze. "I'm not upset with you," he promised huskily. "Please come and sit down." He led her to the rockers positioned in front of the fire hearth.

He settled her in one of the rockers and claimed the other, scooting it nearer. She tensed, ready to bolt.

"Izzy, listen to me—"

"You are angry with me for some reason." She twisted the hem of her nightshift, until a tearing sound made her realize she'd damaged the fine cotton. Hurriedly she untangled herself and smoothed it down.

Sam caught the end of the bunched garment and peeled it away. Brows pinched tight, he fisted her gown hard enough to rip the delicate fabric. At her sharp inhale, he met her gaze. "Honey, I promise my anger is not directed toward you."

"Then what?" Her query was a mere thread of sound in the overly warm room.

Sam's glance dropped to her bared limbs. "I'm enraged at whoever put those caning marks on your legs."

Chapter 12

Horrified, Izzy yanked the hem of her nightshift from Sam's grasp and shoved it over her legs, shamed that he'd seen the marks from the last punishment she'd suffered at her father's hands. That final humiliation had driven her to break a lamp over her brother's head and escape into the night while he lay bleeding all over the carpet.

"Izzy, stop." Sam stilled her fidgeting. "Let go, now. Talk to me." He rubbed soothing circles over her knuckles, a trace of anger still evident in his voice, yet not directed at her.

Slowly, she eased under his touch, relaxing into the rocker cushions, thankful he didn't insist on seeing the full extent of the marks on her. "I don't know where to start," she admitted.

"How about at the beginning?"

Mortification almost weakening her resolve, she stared into the hearth, empty and swept clean for the summer. "You know my father locked me in my room because of my refusal to wed Reginald Dalton."

Sam laid his palm on her knee, covered by her shift. "Some of your injuries are from farther back than a few weeks." He tugged lightly at the hem.

Izzy grasped his wrist to stop him. "Some of them are. My father, he . . ." She swallowed the huge lump in her throat trying to choke her. "He slapped me when I was disobedient as a child. The way most fathers do. He used the c-cane later on."

"How later on?" Sam urged.

Her eyes met his helplessly, drawn to the sympathy she found there. She released his wrist. "After my mother went away, I started fighting him on my duties."

Tamping down her innate modesty, she didn't protest when he slid her shift up her leg and inspected the marks left by Father's most recent caning, along with scars from past transgressions.

With a careful touch, he traced one of the older marks. "How long ago?"

"Two years." Her lips quivered. "I questioned him on the whereabouts of my mother and received my first caning for my insolence." Despite her attempt at stoicism, her shoulders slumped at the horrific memory. "All the while he beat me, he forbade me to ever mention her name again."

Rage burst through Sam like a steam locomotive. It was all he could do not to grab up his holster, tear off to Silver Cache, hunt down William the Third, and give him a taste of his own cane.

His gaze took in the damage to his bride's soft white flesh. Skin like a babe, tender and easily marred. Even after several weeks, the bruises on her neck were still slightly visible.

As fair as she is, the scars might never completely disappear.

Unable to bear the thought of her suffering, Sam rose and scooped her from the rocker, settling back again with her nestled in his lap. She silently curled into his embrace like an abandoned kitten seeking kindness.

Her trust humbled him. He couldn't find the right words to offer comfort, so he let his touch convey his feelings. With one foot he set the rocker in motion, immersed in the feel of her, safe in his arms, her head resting on his shoulder and her silky hair under his chin.

Seconds stretched into minutes as he rocked his new bride, pleased by the way she relaxed fully against him. Tracing over the ruffle edging the neckline of her shift, he wondered where on earth this dainty slip of a girl found the courage needed to bonk her despicable brother over the head with a lamp and run away. Pride swelled within him, picturing the scene in his head.

Recalling her description of how she bested her sibling, an amused snort escaped him.

Izzy raised her head from his shoulder. "What?"

He grinned. "I'm trying to imagine you pounding Willy into the floor with a lamp. Kerosene, I assume? Glass or pewter?"

Her lips curved, revealing a dimple. "Kerosene, made of glass. I think it broke on the way down. Probably spilled everywhere, too."

"And it didn't occur to you to light a matchstick?" She looked askance at him. "Of course it wouldn't, you're far too sweet."

"Well, mostly I liked my curtains. And I had some pretty gowns in my chifferobe. I'd have hated to see them burn," she replied with a straight face.

"There's my girl."

Approval of her feistiness aside, Sam broke out into a sweat at the thought of how the room could have gone up in flames had another lamp been burning, or if a hearth fire had been lit. No matter how well it'd played out, the potential repercussions of her actions drained him of his humor.

"You could have been trapped," he pointed out. "Willy might have found enough strength to stop you from escaping."

Izzy shrugged one slender shoulder. "None of that happened, obviously, because I'm here and well. Thanks to you and most of this town."

Her soft palm against his jaw brought Sam back from the ugly place he'd traveled. Their gazes locked as his hand covered hers. He found such relief in her touch, thankful she'd gotten away and done the smart thing, running to Little Creede.

The rocker slowly came to a halt as his awareness of her, cradled against his bare chest, filled his senses. She was warm beneath the thin gown she wore. Trust and acceptance shone from her eyes, more than enough to build a marriage on.

Every instinct inside him demanded he bed her and seal his claim. *Innocence*, he cautioned. His lips parted on a question—

With a sigh, she relaxed once more. Her sleepy, "Thank you, Sam," only acknowledged his earlier decision that she was nowhere ready to consummate the marriage.

Telling himself he was content to hold her while she slept, Sam set the rocker to motion again.

Birdsong outside the window awoke Izzy from the most restful night she'd enjoyed in many months. She stretched luxuriously, arching her neck to work out any stiffness. Her arms next, one by one, then her legs—

Something pinned down her legs. Something hard and hot beside her.

Almost afraid to look, Izzy turned her head on the pillow, lifting lids encrusted from sleep.

"Oh, my goodness."

Sam lay on his side, an arm flung over her waist where, thankfully, she still wore the borrowed nightshift. One muscled thigh held her in place, underneath blankets rapidly becoming too stifling to leave on. Izzy turned a bit more, curiosity getting the better of her common sense, until she could view more of him.

Lord, he's a handsome man.

He gave no indication her subtle movements had woken him. In the morning light he appeared younger, more carefree, his lashes thick and dark against his cheeks. The white pillow played up the golden tone of his skin, as if the sun itself wrapped around him, smooth and warmer than anything she'd ever felt.

Naked skin.

Insatiably curious to discover how far that bareness might go, she toyed with the edge of the blanket covering her. With the vague recollection of him carrying her to the bed, tucking her in and laying down beside her, Izzy slowly loosened her grip on the blanket. Her new husband might be rough around the edges, but he always remained a gentleman. He'd promised to keep his drawers on while they slept, and she trusted him to keep his word.

She relaxed and burrowed into her pillow, allowing his warmth to lull her back into slumber, unwilling to wake him when he needed his sleep.

"Morning." The rasp at her ear, accompanied by the feel of rough chin-stubble, sent instant shivers through her. "Shh, now. No need to rile yourself, I'm just saying 'morning' is all." Sam's arm tightened around her waist. "Nothing more."

"M-Morning," she managed, trying to tug the blanket higher.

His low chuckle slid across her senses like a caress. "Did you sleep well?"

Izzy nodded. Her mind searched for a witty response, but she came up blank.

"Did you know you talk in your sleep, Missus Singleton?"

"No. No, I didn't." *What on earth did I say?*

His lips hovered near her ear, the warmth of his breath making her pulse race. "You said my name a time or two. Were you dreaming about me, Izzy?"

Izzy wanted to sink into the mattress and never come out. Or jump up and run away. "I don't remember." She tried to move away. "I need to get up."

"No," he said teasingly, "don't think so."

One swift adjustment from her new husband had Izzy almost nose to nose with him.

Uttering a panicked squeak, she glanced down to make sure her gown hadn't ridden up. The blankets obscured the lower half of their bodies. His thigh lay against her bare skin, thankfully covered with what felt like soft cotton. Still, the position was so very intimate.

"I can't—Mister—Sam," she babbled, "we don't know each other well at all."

He tilted his head on the pillow, regarding her somberly. "True. We don't. Doesn't mean we can't learn. Good marriages have been built on less." He stroked a thumb along the corner of her mouth, the gesture tender. His gaze held hers, deep and sure in the lightening room. "I care for you, Izzy. I think we could do very well together."

"You haven't even kissed me." The words flew unconsciously from her mouth. Izzy pinched her lips tight to prevent anything else from slipping past them . . . such as the wild impulse to beg a kiss from him.

A slow smile and a rumbling, "No, I haven't," was all the warning she got, before firm lips teased hers, tasting of morning and manly musk. Her eyes fluttered closed as she sank into her very first kiss.

Sensation bombarded her, from the touch of his tongue at each corner of her mouth, to the hard palms curving along her arms as he lightly traced patterns on her body. Slow and easy despite his coiled muscles, her husband gave instead of demanding from her. When Sam eased her closer, she sighed with delight.

Izzy wasn't stupid. She'd seen enough coupling in the fields to understand the basics, able to make a decent comparison from animal to human. Yet how could she have known the sheer joy of a man enveloping her in his desire, awakening her own?

Head spinning crazily, Izzy clutched his shoulders as she learned how to kiss him back.

He'd jumped aboard riverboats in the dark, won and lost small fortunes, even leapt into murky waters, narrowly missing a churning paddlewheel, after someone accused him of counting cards and pulled a knife on him. Been in fistfights, gunfights, and one actual duel. Kissed his share of women and been seduced countless times.

Nothing could have prepared Sam for the taste of one precious young woman's untried lips. *My wife.*

Soft, sweet, satin-smooth, it was like kissing heaven . . . and he'd barely begun to introduce Izzy to passion. He knew she wasn't ready for anything more than a chaste touch on those lovely lips or careful caresses on her lush body. Temptation threatened to drown him. He couldn't deny himself any longer, not when he had her in the bed with only his cotton drawers and a thin nightshirt separating them.

Just a few kisses, he told himself. It would be enough for now.

Except it wasn't.

He had large, callus-roughened hands. Placing them on her silky flesh seemed almost like sacrilege, yet when he cupped the nape of her neck to hold her more firmly against him, she uttered a soft whimper against his mouth. Offered an opportunity to plumb between her half-parted lips, Sam didn't hesitate and let his tongue stroke hers fully.

Like dipping into pure sunshine.

A voice in the back of his mind told him to stop while he still could. While other girls Izzy's age grew up with decent folks who nurtured and taught, tempered with loving discipline, Izzy had only known heartbreak and pain. She needed time to accustom herself to being a wife.

Still, having her in his arms, her lips beneath his, was more than he could possibly resist. One more kiss, and he'd stop. A final caress, and he'd let her go.

She slid trembling fingers into his hair, and gripped.

And Sam was lost. With a groan, he tugged on the thin ribbon holding together the neckline of her shift, until it came undone. The material slithered down her arm, baring her shoulder and the slope of one rounded, high-tipped breast. The sight of that firm, pink flesh drew him like a lodestone.

One more taste—

"Sam."

"Yeah," he muttered against her rosy skin, kissing his way toward his goal.

"Sam," the muffled voice called, accompanied by hard knocking on wood.

The interruption came from outside their suite.

"Sam, it's Hannah. Please, I need to speak with you right away." Urgency colored her voice.

Izzy stiffened beneath him and wriggled free. Sam dropped his face into the pillow. Telling himself he'd have stopped in a few more seconds didn't help. He knew it wasn't true. It would have been impossible to stop, not with the way Izzy had held on to him and kissed him back.

"Sam, the door."

Sam sighed roughly and rolled to the edge of the bed. Scooping up his discarded trousers, still heaped on the floor where he'd left them the prior evening, he slipped them over his hips and buttoned up haphazardly.

Not meeting his gaze, Izzy picked up his shirt and held it out. After he took it from her, she crawled from bed and retreated to the screen propped in the corner, shielding the privy and tub area of the suite.

Wearily, Sam threw on the shirt and trudged to the door. Unlocking the latch, he swung it open, catching Hannah with her fist raised, ready to knock again. The anxiousness in her eyes had him instantly concerned. "What is it? The babe?"

Hannah wrung her hands. "Forgive me for disturbing you." She dropped her voice. "There are some men here to see you and your bride." Her glance encompassed him and Izzy, who had silently joined him at the open doorway.

He instinctively knew, even as he asked for confirmation. "What men?"

"The ones who came yesterday and disrupted your wedding. They're waiting in the lobby."

At Izzy's gasp, Sam slung an arm around her, pulling her to him. "Don't worry, honey. Nobody is gonna take you away."

"There's one other," Hannah continued. "A Judge from Silver Cache. Wilson, I believe is his name." Her gaze landed on Izzy. "Sweet girl, the judge specifically asked for you."

Chapter 13

With Sam holding tightly to Izzy's hand, they entered the lobby alongside Hannah who immediately hurried to join her husband. Mister Gleason stood near the back of the room, a rifle slung casually across one arm, his vigilant stare locked on the men grouped together, though he greeted his wife warmly. Hannah nestled under his free arm as if used to sharing him with a deadly weapon.

Having her employer there brought Izzy an additional feeling of safety. She'd learned the men of Little Creede were brave and honorable. They'd never let her family force her home.

Her gaze took in the other man Hannah said was a judge from Silver Cache. *Why is he here?* The contract her father waved around yesterday couldn't possibly be legal since they'd forged her signature. *Could it?* Besides, regardless of what her family tried to imply, she was of sound mind. Surely anyone who spoke to her could attest to her sanity.

She stumbled at the thought her marriage could be declared illegal, and she'd be forced into an unwanted union with Reginald Dalton.

Sam steadied her. "Trust me, Izzy. You're completely safe."

Izzy studied the man she'd married. In a very short time she'd learned to not only trust him, but care for him deeply. She took a calming breath. "I do." Her tension eased. "I do trust you, Sam."

He kissed the tip of her nose. "Now, let's see what these reprobates want."

Tickled by his attitude and feeling more confident, she held her head high, meeting her father's unfriendly glower as they covered the remaining distance to the men.

"Finally," her brother ground out hatefully. "Show 'em the damn contract and let's be on our way."

Sam shot Willy a warning glare, making her cowardly sibling drop his eyes. With a final look of disdain toward her brother, he redirected his attention to the man she didn't recognize. "Judge Wilson, what brings you to Silver Cache?"

The judge's gaze held sympathy. "Mister Singleton. I have a contract here signed by the young lady agreeing to wed Mister Dalton in exchange for a generous dowry which has already changed hands."

Before Izzy could deny the claim, Sam stated bluntly, "She said she never signed the document, and even if she had, she's my wife now. No one is going to take her from me."

The words were spoken placidly enough, but there was no missing the threat in Sam's tone or the way his hard assessment swept over the other men.

The judge sighed. "It appears Miss McDougall has emotional issues that Mister Dalton is willing to overlook—"

"Enough," Sam growled. "Did her father tell you how he beat her and locked her away when she refused to marry Dalton?"

Stiffening, Judge Wilson cast her father a disapproving stare. "That's unfortunate, to be sure." He refocused on Sam. "However, it's a parent's right to discipline their child, no matter how abhorrent we may find it to be. The legalities of the contract, and whether your marriage is lawful will have to be worked out in court."

Reginald Dalton spoke up, puffing out his chest with an air of importance. "Until this matter is settled, I believe the best course of action is for Miss McDougall to be placed back with her family."

"Not gonna happen." Sam shifted to block her from the others' view. The fury in his voice and posture indicated he'd defend her from anyone trying to make her leave with them.

Determined to show some backbone, she spoke firmly, peering around Sam's shoulder. "I'm not Miss McDougall any longer." Her statement earned a snort from her father and a scowl of cold ire from Dalton. Izzy held herself tall, taking comfort from Sam's bolstering presence, refusing to use him as a shield.

Hannah slipped quietly from the room, patting her arm as she passed. Silently, Knight took a stance at her side, his rifle steady.

"Don't yew worry yerself, Missus Izzy," he rumbled. "These idjits ain't-a takin' yew from yer home."

Judge Wilson looked like he'd rather be anywhere but there. "I'm sorry, gentlemen." His regard shifted to Knight briefly. "Sending Miss McDougall along with her family might be the best course of action for now."

At Izzy's panicked wheeze, her employer cursed. Sam's lips twisted into a snarl as he gently brought her forward. "Izzy, show the fine judge your legs."

"W-What?" she stuttered, her gaze flying to his.

"Remember, you promised me your trust." Tenderly, he nuzzled her temple. "Please show the judge your legs."

Her father's angry voice broke in rudely. "I don't know what that has to do with anything." He flapped a hand at her brother. "Willy, get your sister so we can leave."

The click of Knight Gleason cocking his weapon stopped Willy in his tracks. "Ah wouldn't come no closer, suh. Though ah use the title loosely, yew understand." He thumbed the stock. "Yew know, ah could git mahself in a heap of trouble if'n mah finger slipped." Knight bared his teeth in a parody of a grin.

The embarrassment of having to reveal how she'd been mistreated at her father's hands sent a burst of heat from Izzy's neck to her scalp. Eyes downcast, she lifted her skirts high enough for the judge to view the relatively new welts as well as the older marks from her two years of beatings. Only her father knew how far up those scars actually went.

The judge inhaled sharply.

Izzy quickly dropped her skirt and turned into her husband's embrace, burrowing against his shirt.

"Shh. It's all right." He cupped a hand around her nape and held her close. "Have you seen enough, sir?" he asked the judge.

"Yes, son. I do believe I have." Amid the grumblings of both her father and Willy, as well as Reginald Dalton threatening to bring a lawsuit against the court and everyone involved, the judge ordered, "Miss McDougall—"

"Singleton," Sam barked out. "*Missus* Singleton."

"Yes, yes of course," Judge Wilson said apologetically. "Missus Singleton appears to be quite happy and safe where she is. Unless you can bring proof of her involvement in criminal activity to cheat Mister Dalton for the money exchanged in this alleged contract you claim she signed, this case, in my legal opinion, is closed."

Sam held on to Izzy, fresh rage eclipsing him as he stared at the man who'd put those marks on her soft skin. As much as he wanted to send a bullet straight into her father's cold heart, he couldn't keep her safe if he rotted in prison for murder. At least the coward had the brains to retreat under Sam's hot stare.

"What?" Willy burst out, raising a fist to shake it in the air. "We came for Isadora and we're not leaving without her."

Knight Gleason moved so fast, it even surprised Sam. The large gambler was quite nimble on his feet.

"Listen heah, yew lil' pissant. This young miss is wed to mah right-hand man. She's also mah employee, and theahfo' under mah protection. Try takin' her outta heah, an' yew'll be meetin' yer maker faster than yew kin say 'Lawd forgive me, for ah have sinned.'"

In that moment, Willy very much resembled his father as all the color drained from his face and he gulped. Sam's lip curled in disdain. Craven, the both of them, using their bullying tactics on an innocent young woman like Izzy.

The temper Sam had managed to contain—so far—boiled over. "Get out of this town and don't come back. If I see you again, the only way you'll be leaving is in a wooden box."

"Yew heard the man," Knight barked when the three only stood there like dummies. "Git!"

Reginald Dalton adjusted his fancy string tie. "Fine, we'll leave." His casual tone didn't match the cold anger in his eyes when they met Sam's. "For now. Keep in mind, I'm a rich man with powerful connections, and I *will* see the contract enforced."

In a blink, Sam drew his Colt, aiming dead center to Dalton's forehead. "The hell you will."

Wilson cleared his throat. "Now, there's no need for violence." He strode for the exit. "Come along, gentlemen. I have other demands today and need to return to Silver Cache. We're done here."

Dalton's mouth thinned to a white line. Without another word he spun away and strode after the judge. Sam remained at the ready, in case the arrogant dandy changed his mind and decided to go for his weapon, while both the McDougall men scurried to keep up with him.

Knight started after them. "Ah'll make sure the scallywags leave town."

"Sam, what are we going to do?" The dismay in Izzy's voice increased his frustration at how she feared her family would win and she'd be forced to wed Dalton.

Over my dead carcass. Or theirs, if need be.

Shielding his emotions, he made sure to show only calmness when he turned back to her. He'd never allow this amazing young woman to be forced into the bed of a monster. Izzy deserved to be well-loved by a man who cared for her, and Sam had every intention of being that man.

"They're bluffing, honey. Their false contract can't be enforced. You're my wife, and nothing on God's green earth will change that."

The sound of a door opening brought Sam's attention to Hannah, padding slowly across the polished floor. Her eyes held worry though her smile was as bright as ever.

"Why don't you go with Hannah?" Sam gave his wife a brief hug and kissed her cheek. "I need to drop by the jail and speak with Joshua."

Hannah took Izzy's hand. "C'mon, sweet girl. Let's go see if Dolores needs help in the kitchen."

Izzy's eyes, darker than usual in the afternoon light, locked on him, and he felt humbled by the trust he read there. "Thank you."

"Nothing to thank me for." Unable to resist, he kissed her again, this time on her soft mouth. "I won't be long. Go on, now."

Ten minutes later, Sam entered the jailhouse to find Joshua talking with Ben.

"Howdy, Sam," Ben said. "You just saved me a trip to the Galleria to fetch you."

Sam arched a brow, his gaze shifting to Joshua. "What for?"

Lang's expression didn't bode well for the upcoming conversation. "Robert Blackwood and his missus stopped by earlier with some information she discovered."

"What sort of information?"

Ben spoke up. "We think we've figured out why Izzy's menfolk are so damn fired up about her marrying Dalton."

"That's never going to happen," Sam snapped.

"And *there's* the issue, Sam," Joshua stressed. "You're the only thing stopping her family from getting what they want. I think you need to watch your back."

"You believe they'll come after me? For what reason? Maybe you'd better share what you think I need to know."

"Yeah." Joshua waved at a wooden chair in front of his desk.

Ben strode toward the door. "I'll check on things around town, Sheriff. Take your time."

"Thanks, Ben." Joshua took a seat at his desk.

Sam pulled the visitor's chair over. "Tell me what you know."

"Maggie Blackwood suspects one of the McDougall men has a gambling problem. A serious one."

"What makes her think that?"

"Izzy's family doesn't own the home they live in. It's rented. Her father recently tried to take out a bank loan to buy it but couldn't come up with enough money. One of the barkeeps at that new watering hole in Silver Cache complained to Robert about William getting drunk and then losing money at poker. Happened more than a few times and led to this fellow banning William from his place. Apparently the elder McDougall tried to get gambling credit based on money a 'friend' of his would pay him. Insisted it was coming to him any day now, McDougall's exact words."

"You think McDougall is bargaining away his daughter in exchange for money from Dalton?"

"Crossed my mind, considering the man clearly has a gambling problem. Seen it plenty in my time."

Sam rolled his shoulders back to ease the tension centered there. "I suppose that could be it. Though it still doesn't explain why Dalton wants her so badly."

Joshua shifted uncomfortably. "She's a beautiful woman, Sam. It could be nothing more than that."

"She is. Beautiful and sweet and caring. Still, they've gone through a lot of trouble to get her wed to Dalton." Sam frowned, rubbing his jaw thoughtfully. "My gut's telling me there's something more at play here, and we need to find out what it is."

Chapter 14

"I have something for you."

Looking up from the pot she stirred, Izzy met Sam's gaze. With a half-smile, he leaned against the wall next to the stove.

Wiping her hands on her apron, her stomach fluttered under his regard. He held out a small box for her, and her pulse raced with excitement. It'd been so long since she'd received a gift from anyone.

"For me?" Glancing around the room, she spotted Dolores industriously kneading dough at the bread counter, humming under her breath, while Luellen sat on the floor beneath the window and played with two rag dolls dressed as a lady and gent. Neither paid any mind to her or Sam.

"Take it," he urged.

She scrutinized the box, made of dark wood, worn-looking and rounded at the edges. Hesitantly she reached for it, and he laid it on her palm. It felt smooth and warm.

"Open it, honey. It won't bite."

Slowly, Izzy lifted the lid. And gasped at what she found, nestled against a bit of lambswool. "It's a ring." Confused, she raised her eyes to Sam's. "It's lovely."

She lifted the band from its soft nest and held it to the light coming in from the window. Creamy seed pearls framed a single, square-cut amethyst. She turned it so the deep lavender gem sparkled. "I've never seen anything so beautiful."

"It's Russian gold." Sam took her left hand and eased off the signet ring from their wedding day. "My mother was Russian." He slid the amethyst in its place, the fit almost perfect. "Her family worked in gold and jewels. This ring was a gift from my grandmother, to my mother. She never took it off, until . . ."

Izzy regarded him worriedly. "Sam?"

He blinked. "It's not important." He kissed the back of her hand. "Happy Birthday, Missus Singleton."

"My birthday was almost a week ago," she protested.

"Does that mean I have to take back the ring?" He grabbed playfully.

Izzy snatched her hand back. "No, I love it."

"As a wedding ring?" Sam trailed a finger down her jaw.

Mindful of the audience in the corner—Dolores and Luellen both avidly looking on—Izzy nodded shyly. "It's the perfect wedding ring." She rose on tiptoes and brushed a kiss on his cheek. "Thank you, Sam. I'll never take it off."

He wrapped his arms around her in the overly warm kitchen. Izzy flushed at Dolores's knowing laugh as the woman hustled Luellen from the room, affording them some privacy.

Sam brought his lips to her ear. "We've been married four days. You know what that means, don't you?"

Three days ago, she'd moved from her small room on the first floor of the Galleria into his more expansive and luxurious quarters upstairs, a suite with its own sitting room and separate water closet. Hannah had helped her settle in, directing the addition of a ladies' vanity and chifferobe for the gowns and assorted garments lent to Izzy her first day here.

She flushed, recalling how she'd slept in Sam's arms; quite comfortably, in fact. Innocently. Unsure what to say in response to her husband's teasing question, Izzy swallowed against a dry throat. "It's time to change the bedsheets?"

Smug *and* handsome, mischief in his dark eyes, his rich chuckle vibrated against her. "No, it means I'm lagging behind in my wedded duties. I would greatly enjoy taking you out to dinner. The Stage House puts on a fine meal."

"You would?" At his arched brows, Izzy wanted to kick herself for sounding like a child barely out of her pinafores, and hastily amended, "Dinner at the Stage House would be delightful, Mister Samuel."

"Just Sam," he reminded her, tweaking her nose.

"All right. Dinner at the Stage House would be delightful." She paused, then teasingly murmured, "Just Sam."

Willy bit off the end of his cigar and spat it on the rug.

Glaring at the wet chunk of tobacco, Reginald Dalton's lip curled in disgust. "That is an original Aubusson, boy. Pick up your rubbish and dispose of it properly."

Scratching the tip of a matchstick on the sole of his boot, Willy lit the cigar and expelled a cloud of smoke. "Don't call me boy," he warned, shifting the fat cigar from one side of his mouth to the other. Letting the matchstick burn down until it went out, he dropped it on the rug, waiting for Dalton to explode. Feeling ornery, Willy ground the burnt ashes into the thick wool.

"For pity's sake, Willy, stop antagonizing our benefactor," his father admonished. Slumped in an armchair with his bony legs stuck out in front of him, the man had been drinking steadily since their return from Little Creede two days ago. Willy doubted he'd eaten more than a bite here and there.

"He's not *my* benefactor." Willy flung himself onto the sofa, which creaked ominously. Ignoring Dalton, standing by the fireplace with clenched fists, he flicked ash, uncaring where it landed. "And I'm not a damned maid. Isadora'll clean it up when she comes back."

"She's not coming back, you fool," his father yelled, trying to sit upright on his chair, clutching the table nearby to steady himself. "You think that bunch at the casino's gonna give her up? Hell, by now the sumbitch who married her has probably bedded her plenty."

"You should've let me start shooting," Willy began, thrusting out his chest intimidatingly. "One shot and I'd have grabbed her—"

Before he could finish his boast, Dalton's furious glare landed on him. With an ugly twist on his lips, he strode to the sofa. Willy shrank back into the cushions warily.

"Your stupidity defies description." Dalton propped his hands on the back of the sofa to cage Willy in. "Our Judge Wilson is a pious one. You'd be in jail awaiting trial if you'd gotten off a shot. And I'd trust your loyalty to your father—and me—about as far as I could toss your worthless hide." He shoved away and paced, leaving Willy to blot the sweat from his brow with a shirtsleeve.

"Bastard," he muttered.

Dalton spun and stalked back to the sofa. "Yes, I'm a bastard," he hissed. "I also seem to be the only one willing to do what it takes to regain Isadora."

"Which is?" Willy stared up at the man hovering over him, longing to punch him until his nostrils bled out.

"Eliminate my so-called competition." Dalton sneered. "What else?"

Sam silently entered the room, enjoying the way his bride turned this way and that as she viewed herself in the beveled mirror.

So beautiful. Recalling the scruffy, dirt-stained pantry thief of a short time ago, he was amazed at how far she had already come. Still somewhat shy and reluctant to speak up for herself, Izzy had nevertheless become the lovely young woman she was always meant to be.

The gown she wore accentuated her tiny waist and sloping shoulders, its deep blue complimenting her eyes. Smiling, he enjoyed the way she pleated the skirts and held them out, swishing the material to and fro. When she caught him staring, she pinkened.

"Hello," she mumbled, tucking her hands behind her back. The movement arched her spine, and Sam's focus latched on to the swell of her breasts under the form-fitting bodice. Catching the direction of his gaze, fresh color stained her cheeks.

Wanting to put her at ease, he offered a smile. "You look stunning, Izzy. With you on my arm, I'll be the envy of everyone."

Izzy ducked her head and toyed with a sleeve. "It's the dress. Watered silk is so beautiful." She traced along a section of lace. "Vivian brought it over earlier, said she'd probably never wear it." She raised her head and met Sam's eyes. "Who gives things like this away to a complete stranger?"

"Little Creede is a generous town. And you are no longer a stranger here." Sam offered his arm, relieved when she took it willingly. Like a skittish colt stretching her legs for the first time, his shy bride had begun to blossom. After he'd presented her with his mother's ring, the quick kiss she'd placed on his cheek had been the first time she had taken the initiative in showing him affection. Sam planned on drawing her out, little by little, until she felt secure in their marriage.

As he led her down the wide staircase toward the lobby of the Galleria, she gave him an encompassing glance. "You look very nice, Sam."

Her praise meant a lot, and he leaned in for a quick nuzzle of her hair as they paused on the landing. "Why, thank you, ma'am."

Sam hated dressing up, but her reaction to his black superfine dinner coat and trim cuffed trousers made up for the hot fabric causing him to sweat as they strolled to the Stage House. He'd rip it off and roll up his sleeves, first chance he got. For now, Sam basked in her admiration.

Folks passed them on the boardwalk, their smiles and greetings brightening Izzy's eyes until they shone. The late-afternoon sun laid a glimmer over her dark curls, and he was glad she hadn't bothered with a hat. Izzy's lack of feminine affectation was one of the things Sam treasured the most about her.

Catherine Carter met them at the Stage House door with her young daughter Charity balanced on her hip. "Welcome to the Miner Stage House, Missus Izzy. It's about time your husband brought you around for Sunday dinner." She winked at Sam while Charity babbled and held out pudgy arms. "You'd better take her, Sam. You can't keep a besotted female waiting."

Obligingly, Sam released Izzy's elbow and gathered up the tot. She immediately stuck a wet thumb in his ear. "Rascal," he mock-growled, earning him a giggle as she laid her reddish-blond head on his shoulder and gazed up at him. "I suppose you'll want all the biscuits."

That perked her up, fast. "Bee-kee!" She bounced in his embrace.

"I can take her back," Catherine offered.

Sam shook his head. "Nah, I'll keep her a while. Having two lovely ladies to dine with makes me a lucky man." He glanced over at his bride. "Missus Izzy, will you share me with this young dickens?"

"Of course." Amusement colored her tone.

Catherine seated them at a front table where Charity could wave at incoming diners. Not a particular enthusiast of children, Sam had found himself enchanted by the tiny girl who already had half the town wrapped around her dainty finger. And for some reason she seemed to like Sam a great deal, breaking out in a smile every time she spotted him.

He didn't envy her daddy's protectiveness when Charity grew up and started attracting boys like honey. Frank would be in for the battle of his life, trying to beat off the beaux sniffing around his daughter, already a flirt at barely fifteen months.

He gripped her diapered bottom to keep her steady and caught Izzy staring at him. He lifted a quizzical brow. "Yes?"

"You're sweet with her." She eyed him curiously. "You don't seem like—never mind."

Sam easily guessed her thoughts. "I don't seem like the kind to tolerate noisy children."

"Sorry, I shouldn't have said anything."

Sam winked at her. "Well, you would be right." Charity released a soft breath against his neck. He stroked her wispy curls, musing, "I lived on a riverboat for years. Gaming and roulette was a poor choice for a family's future. Never thought I'd marry. Or like tots all that much." He repositioned her as she played with the buttons on his vest. "Maybe having a few of these heathens wouldn't be such a bad idea."

He might have teased her further, except he spotted Dolores Lund coming toward their table with a cake. "Right on time," he murmured.

"What?" Izzy twisted to follow his gaze. Her eyes grew wide and wondering.

Sam let Charity slip to her feet, the child's attention now on the cake Dolores set in front of Izzy. "Can you tell Missus Izzy 'Happy Birthday,' Charity?"

The child toddled to Izzy and grabbed her skirts to steady herself. "Ha ba, ha ba!" She clapped her hands, before one shot out toward the white icing swirled over the top and sides of the cake. "Me."

"Not you, young missy." Dolores scooped her up. "You had yours a few months back." She addressed Izzy fondly. "Many happy returns, my dear."

Somehow a simple Sunday dinner had become a party in her honor.

Sam did all of this for me. Izzy couldn't believe her husband's kindness. And he'd involved half the town, too.

Tender beef with brown gravy ladled over pan biscuits, and a large piece of her wonderful birthday cake was followed by all the dining salon patrons raising their glasses to her in a toast. There were gifts, too, much to Izzy's surprise. A lovely walking skirt and high-necked blouse from Catherine. Two of the dearest hats from Millie Pierce, who owned a milliner shop in town. Small tokens of hand-embroidered handkerchiefs and tatted gloves, even a parasol, things she'd never have thought to obtain for herself. Each gift touched her deeply.

A heavily bearded older man, introducing himself as Dub, had serenaded her with a fiddle while she and Sam ate.

After their meal Sam rose from his seat and held out his hand. "Will you dance with me, Izzy?"

"Yes, of course."

Full of delicious food and warmed by everyone's good wishes, she lost her usual reticence in her husband's arms. He waltzed her slowly around tables and chairs, the poignant melody of "Down in the Valley" swirling in her head with each turn. They passed Knight and Hannah at one table, his massive palm engulfing hers as her head bobbed to the notes Dub coaxed from his fiddle.

Others had taken to dancing, as Dub finessed one song into another with ease. Harrison Carter waltzed by, a daughter in each arm, while at another table Retta sat with her newborn daughter, Quinn, a name Izzy found quite lovely. Next to Retta, her mother-by-marriage, Lucinda Blackwood, snuggled the twin boys, one on each knee. The beautiful woman didn't look old enough to be the matriarch of the Carter family.

"Are you having a good time?" Sam's low question tickled her ear, and she shivered in reaction.

She raised her eyes to his, melting at the warmth and tenderness she found there. "I'm having the best time. Thank you for this, Sam. For all of this."

He grinned. "These folks do appreciate any reason for a get together. In fact—"

A sharp cry rent the music and broke into whatever he'd been about to say. Stopping in mid-swing, they both turned toward where Hannah had been sitting with Knight.

Now she stood, bent over, one arm wrapped around herself. "K-Knight." Her voice quavered.

Her husband's arm snapped around her shoulders, his expression panicked.

"My water broke," she moaned. "You'd best fetch the doc."

Chapter 15

"Alexander Knight Gleason," Izzy announced.

"I like it," Sam drawled. Lounging on the rocker by the fireplace, he watched as she finished arranging their clean linens in the bottom drawer of the chifferobe.

She ducked behind the privy screen to change into her nightclothes. "I do, too. Such a nice name."

Hannah and babe now rested comfortably in their suite, doted on by a very proud Knight. When not caught up in her regular duties in the Galleria kitchen, Izzy had spent a portion of the rainy day helping Hannah fold numerous cotton flannel squares into diapers.

When she stepped back into the main room, Sam patted his knee. "Come have a seat, honey."

Trying not to stare at her husband's bare chest, Izzy gingerly perched on his lap. The low-burning logs in the fireplace took the dampness from the room while Sam's body heat warmed her in a completely different way. By concentrating on the flames instead, she relaxed enough to share bits and pieces about the newest Gleason. "I got to hold him for a bit. He's so tiny. Has a bold shock of red hair. I'd wager he'll be tall like his father." She grinned. "The rest of him is all Hannah. He's already got her delicate facial features. Master Alexander will grow up to be a heartbreaker, mark my words."

Amusement crinkled the corners of Sam's eyes. "Knight's been strutting around the Galleria like a proud peacock, boasting about his new son and praising his wife."

At his fond tone, a wave of affection welled up inside her for the husband she was fast coming to adore. Though their union had started out for all the wrong reasons, she couldn't imagine being married to anyone else. When she'd been holding Alexander earlier, enjoying the feel of him snuggled against her, the image of an infant boy with sunshine hair and deep brown eyes like Sam's had blazed across her mind.

She chewed on her bottom lip, in a quandary about what she should do next. They slept in the same bed every night, and Sam had been the perfect gentleman. Izzy didn't know the first thing about seduction, too shy to ask him to make her a real wife with everything the marital bed entailed.

"What's wrong?"

The words, "I want a babe of my own," fell from her lips. *Oh, my God.* She broke out in a hot flush of embarrassment. "I-I mean—"

At his burst of laughter, she pinched her mouth tight against the sudden hurt she felt. Was the idea of having a child with her so ridiculous? The dream, that this could someday be a real marriage, shriveled and died.

Sam had only married her to protect her, because he was a good man . . . not because he wanted to spend the rest of his life with her.

"I'm sorry, I don't know what I was thinking. Such a stupid thing to say." She jumped to her feet. "This marriage isn't real."

As she turned to flee, Sam clasped her upper arm and tugged. Izzy tumbled back onto his lap, her legs hanging off to one side.

"Not true," he murmured.

She kept her gaze averted, humiliated by her outburst. She hadn't missed the hint of frustration in his voice. How many times had her father corrected her for her impulsive ways? Her stomach tightened at the memories.

Sam rubbed one hand up and down her back. "Will you look at me?"

She shook her head, lowering her chin to her chest.

"Please." He didn't force her, only quietly waited.

Finally, she lifted her head and met his tender gaze.

"Izzy, I wasn't laughing at the thought of having a child with you. I laughed because you looked so shocked at the words coming out of your pretty mouth. I want you to know, this marriage will be a real one."

Her brows drew together. Sam didn't love her, so staying with her forever made no sense. "Why—"

"Shh. Let me finish."

Izzy's hopes rose. Did he want what she'd already hoped for?

"I care for you a great deal, Izzy."

"You do?" she squeaked out.

"I think we have a chance at something good here. And someday I would like to have a houseful of children."

"With me?" *What a ridiculous question.* She bit her lower lip to stop herself from saying anything else.

"Do you see another wife anywhere?" he teased gently.

Unable to form a coherent thought, Izzy swallowed. The way Sam watched her did strange things to her. The oddest feeling of need grew within her as her breasts tingled, their buds overly sensitive.

She squirmed on his lap. Her eyes widened when his manhood swelled beneath her bottom, a groan spilling from his lips. "Oh, my."

"Shall we start trying tonight, Missus Singleton?"

Izzy's pulse thrummed with both nervousness and excitement. She very much wanted to become Sam's wife in every sense of the word. There was only one problem.

"Would we . . . need to undress?"

Sam blinked. *Not the words I'd expect next from my new bride.* "Removing of clothes is normally involved."

A rosy flush stained Izzy's cheeks. "I see."

Her reticence gave him pause, because she didn't exactly sound shy, as he would have expected from an innocent young woman. Rather, melancholy echoed in her reply.

Knots formed in his gut. Why would the thought of being naked with him make her sad?

"You've got to know I'd never force you."

Izzy's beautiful eyes widened. "Of course I do, Sam. That's not it at all."

His brows wrinkled. "Then what is it?"

She pulled away and hopped off his lap, beginning to pace. As much as he wanted to go to her, he needed her to make the decision to trust him with whatever had her so upset.

After what seemed like an eternity, she stopped and faced him with a look of determination, then spoke in a rush, forcing the words out as if each one hurt. "The marks on my legs from Father's canings aren't the only scars on my body."

Instant fury ignited inside him. He shot to his feet, fists clenched, as images of this sweet woman being beaten boiled in his mind.

Damned if I'll see my wife haunted by such cruel treatment.

If her father had been present, Sam would have murdered the bastard with his bare hands. Grinding his back teeth together, he fought for control of the emotions he'd kept buried for so many years, yet they thrashed at him.

All during his childhood, Sam had endured cruelty from those who delighted in lording power over the weak. Shoved onto an orphan train at thirteen, heading to hell-only-knew where, undernourished and clutching his mother's ring, he'd hid the treasure in his smalls to keep from losing it or having it stolen. It'd been the only thing he had left of the beautiful, broken woman who'd fled Russia as a young widowed mother and died before she could secure the 'better American life' she had promised him.

It wasn't until fear entered Izzy's eyes and she shrank back that he managed to pull himself together. Shamed he'd frightened her, he wrestled down his inner demons and vowed to someday make William the Third pay for every ounce of pain inflicted on her.

"I'm sorry, honey. I'm not upset with you. I'm upset *for* you." Sam slowly approached, relieved when she didn't retreat. Instead, she nestled against him, her head under his chin. "Do you want to tell me?"

Her silence prompted Sam to lift her into his arms and sit on the bed. Reclining against the headboard, he cradled her protectively. "You can share this with me, Izzy."

He waited, determined not to pressure her.

"All right," came her whispered reply. Not meeting his gaze, she folded her hands primly in her lap. "I told you how the abuse began after Mother's disappearance."

He remembered the conversation well. His anger over what he'd learned that day had yet to diminish, and this new information only made him more resolved to keep her out of her family's miserable grip. "Yeah, I do."

"About six months ago, my father's anger escalated. I'm not sure why. About the same time, Reginald Dalton arrived in Silver Cache for a visit and Father invited him to stay at our house. I was made to join them for evening supper. After cooking the meal," she added with a sigh, "I sat at the table as they ate and drank. One night I refused and it made Father furious."

"What did he do?" Sam spoke as calmly as he could manage.

She didn't immediately respond. His tension grew with each second that passed.

Finally, she broke the silence. "My first few beatings were on my back. After that, Father only used the cane on my legs when I acted contrary or displeased him." Her lower lip trembled. "But the night I wouldn't dine with Reginald, Father beat my back again, harder than ever."

"Izzy—"

She continued as if lost in the past. "Reginald returned to Chicago a few days after my beating. Father stopped punishing me, only slapping me when he found my disposition contrary. I didn't think Reginald would come back to Silver Cache, but he did, months later. And I refused Father's demands again."

Her breath hitched on a broken sigh. "He put his hands around my neck and threatened to choke me if I didn't obey him. That's when he locked me in my room without food or water."

"Jesus Lord." Sam's heart broke at Izzy's desolation. Caning was a horribly vicious punishment. But throttling his own child . . . Knowing she had been tortured so by her father brought such grief to mind, for a moment it eclipsed Sam's anger. If he could go back in time and take her unfair punishment upon himself, he would. "It pains me to think this happened to you. Will you show me?"

A long moment of silence stretched into two, until she finally answered in such a soft voice, he had to lean in to hear her. "All right."

She straightened, twisting until her back was to him. Silently, she unlaced the bodice of her nightgown. With a shake of her shoulders, the soft cotton pooled around her waist.

Seeing the evidence of her father's cruelty, Sam sucked in a harsh breath. He clenched his jaw to stop the snarl clogging his throat, unwilling to upset or frighten her.

Caning marks, some not fully healed, streaked across her shoulders, three on the right side. A few more overlapped on the left.

"Do they hurt?"

"No. Not any longer."

He studied the rest of the ravages done to her porcelain skin. Lighter marks from the older beatings covered the lower half of her back, at least half a dozen. Some were barely visible, others more pronounced. And unfortunately, his beautiful wife was correct. Though many of the scars would eventually fade, the newer, deeper marks were bad enough to remain, perhaps for the rest of her life.

Forcing down his rage, Sam swept a palm across her back, tracing the edges of the thickest scar. "I promise, no one will ever do this to you again."

She adjusted the gown's bodice to cover her shoulders and turned to him. "I believe you, Sam."

Her trust humbled him, and unable to resist, he kissed her. When she parted her lips, he slid his tongue inside to explore her velvet recesses, coaxing an answering response from her. Each kiss increased his desire until he had to pull back or else risk losing control completely.

As much as Sam wanted to make love to her, he'd never do anything to cause her a moment of remorse. She'd already been hurt too many times in her young life, and he didn't want to add to her burden. Izzy would only know kindness and contentment from him.

Her dazed expression pleased him. The woman stole more of his heart each day.

"Sam?" She attempted to pull him in for another kiss.

He resisted, even as everything inside him told him to claim her. He'd never desired to bed a woman more than he did his new bride right now.

She was a vision. Full lips reddened from his kisses, hair mussed, eyes bright with a need he reckoned she didn't even understand.

The woman appeared ready to be thoroughly loved.

Sam wasn't quite convinced. "Are you sure this is what you want?"

"Yes."

"Izzy, we have our entire lives ahead of us. I don't want you to feel—"

She placed two fingers against his lips, silencing him. "For a long time I've known my father would choose a husband for me, regardless of my feelings. Resigning myself to my fate didn't stop me from dreaming of the kind of man I hoped to marry someday." Her breath hitched, and his name rolled off her tongue like a prayer. "Sam, that man is you."

He searched her face, looking for the truthfulness of her words. Trust and caring stared back at him, along with a good dose of nervousness and hesitation.

She's not ready. Tonight wouldn't be the night he claimed his wife. He needed to ease her into the ways of lovemaking first.

He nibbled her ear. "Will you trust me to know what you need?"

Izzy nodded.

She hadn't yet refastened her nightgown, enabling Sam to slide his hands over her shoulders, loosening the bodice until it once again fell to her waist, baring her creamy breasts to his view. They were beautifully formed, pale and pink-tipped. He cupped one in each palm, delighting in the rounded handfuls. His thumb grazed across her tight nipples, eliciting a dulcet purr from his bride.

Readjusting their position, he eased her onto the mattress and settled over her, his hard length pulsing against the thin fabric shielding her thighs. Covering her mouth in a soft kiss, he flexed his hips, putting pressure right where he knew she needed it the most. Her shocked gasp made him smile against her lips. Without even realizing it, Izzy accepted his call, her legs falling open so he could get closer still.

Sam continued to make love to her mouth while caressing her breasts. All the while, he rubbed against the sensitive spot at the apex of her thighs. The scent of her passion blossomed, her keening moans growing louder as she allowed herself to take pleasure from him.

Finally, Sam broke their kiss and trailed his mouth to her breast, tonguing a taut peak, before nipping it with his teeth.

"Oh." Izzy clasped his head against her quivering flesh. "What am I—what's happening?"

"Relax, honey." Sam kissed the swell of her other breast, then reached for the edge of her gown to lift the material to her waist. Rolling his tongue around her hardened nipple, he slid his hand to the damp cleft between her legs and flicked the tender bud centered there.

Izzy all but flew off the bed, her slender frame arching beneath him. Her ragged mewls of delight indicated his wife would be a receptive lover. Sam's groin throbbed with the need to bury himself inside her. Acknowledging she was untouched, and thus required more time to adjust to the idea of being with him, was the only thing stopping him from taking everything from her.

"So beautiful," he murmured.

With her cheeks flushed and her breathing uneven, she appeared to be near her peak. If he could get her there, it would help ease the way for when he eventually took her the first time. Concentrating on making his wife feel good, Sam slowly penetrated her with two fingers. Sweat dampened his brow from the effort of keeping his own lust under control. For now, he'd gladly suffer unrequited desire.

Unconsciously urging him on, Izzy raised her hips while he carefully stretched her inner walls, her slick heat clinging to his fingers. Giving her only a moment to adjust to the feel of him petting her from within, he withdrew slowly before plunging in again, setting up a shallow rhythm as her chants of, "Don't stop, don't stop, please don't stop," let him know she enjoyed what he did to her. Shaking with need, Sam circled his thumb against her sensitive button.

Shuddering under his touch, Izzy's cries of satisfaction echoed around the bedroom.

Chapter 16

Alexander Knight Gleason blinked while he fed, finally falling asleep against his mama's breast—after a single, long belch—and simply melted Izzy's heart as she sat in a rocking chair pulled up near the bed, watching Hannah tenderly cup his downy head.

Knight stood at her shoulder, stroking her loose hair. "Ah have been blessed by the Almighty hisself, ain't I?" Though he spoke to Izzy, his entire focus remained on his family, as well it should. "Mah boy'll take after his daddy."

"I believe you're correct, sir," Izzy teased. It was impossible not to find the blustering Galleria owner exceedingly charming, as he fussed over his wife and stared adoringly at the tiny babe in her arms.

"Would you like to hold him, Izzy?" Hannah offered. Clear-eyed and cheery despite only giving birth a few days ago, nevertheless she moved restlessly about on the mattress. Izzy figured she had to be sore, unable to get fully comfortable. And Hannah still needed to rest whenever her child did, especially after a nursing session.

"I'd love to get in a snuggle." Izzy eagerly held out her hands, and Knight scooped up his son, settling the minuscule, linen-wrapped bundle securely in her arms. While he retreated to sit next to Hannah, she savored the precious little mite slumbering against her, yawning now and then, one tiny hand opening and closing as if searching for his mother. "He's the most beautiful thing I have ever seen," she whispered, rocking him carefully.

"Yew want one of yer own, ah'd bet." Knight winked at her. "Ain't nothin' more'n gettin' started."

"Knight, don't embarrass the girl," Hannah chided, her gaze knowing as she noted Izzy's discomfort. "Don't you pay my man any mind, dear. Babes take root when they're ready, and not a moment sooner."

"Um, certainly." Izzy cleared her throat. She set the chair to rocking again as the infant woke and began fussing. He quieted immediately, falling asleep with his rosebud mouth open, emitting a trickle of milky drool. Relaxing into the cushions, her thoughts drifted while Knight and Hannah chatted in low tones.

Finally, the new mother dozed off.

Izzy lightly rubbed Alexander's back. "Hannah should nap as much as possible."

"Ah think so, too. Yew know mah bride is a touch stubborn." Knight kissed his sleeping wife's head and caressed her arm. "Neveh thought ah'd be this lucky in mah life. Yew'll see, once yew an' Sam git yerselves settled an' start poppin' out young'uns."

Fresh heat burst over Izzy at the kindly, emotional words from her employer. Sinking down into the rocker, she hummed a lullaby under her breath to distract herself, yet images came hard and fast, completely improper given she held an innocent babe.

Last night, she'd been certain her husband would make her a true wife, the mysteries of the marriage bed finally revealed. It hadn't happened quite the way she'd expected. Still, she'd awoken content this morning, hoping Sam would continue where he'd so obviously left off.

She'd found the space next to her empty, the sheets cool with only an indentation in his pillow to assure he'd slept with her all night. Vaguely she'd recalled a kiss to her forehead and a low, "Sleep, honey," whispered in her ear.

Pushing away her disappointment, Izzy rose carefully and crossed the sunlit room, placing Alexander in his father's arms. "I've got to head down and start work. Please let me know if Hannah needs anything."

"Well now, ah understand mah Magnolia plans on stoppin' by later on, but thank yew kindly, Missus Izzy." Knight produced a dazzling smile. "Yew come on back up wheneveh yew want."

Hannah's got to be one of the luckiest women alive.

Izzy smiled in return and exited the Gleasons' suite. Taking the back stairs to the kitchen a floor below, she reminded herself she was lucky as well. Sam was affectionate, strong, fair-minded, and protective. She glanced down at the lovely ring once belonging to his mother. Of all the women he could have picked to receive such an heirloom, he'd chosen her. Surely, if he'd never intended for their vows to be lasting, he wouldn't have done it.

She'd been afraid Sam would turn away in disgust from her scars. Instead, she'd seen tightly contained fury on her behalf, along with a strong dose of worry over any lingering discomfort she might be having.

Love had sparked inside her, a small glow of hope and happiness Izzy would cherish and nourish as they built a life together. She prayed her husband would someday return those feelings.

Pausing on the last stair, she clasped the kitchen latch, then hesitated, thinking furiously. Though he'd touched her in ways she'd never dreamed possible, he'd chosen not to make her fully his wife.

Her confidence wavered.

Why had he stopped, if not for her scars? Did he consider her too young to be a wife?

That must be it.

Izzy desperately wanted the 'real' marriage Sam had talked about last night. And she needed to convince him she was old enough, ready enough. Filled with determination, she squared her shoulders and swung the door open.

Somehow, she'd win Sam's affections and prove to him that he'd made the right choice when he'd married her.

"Here's a nice spot." Sam pointed to a cleared area underneath a sprawling ponderosa. "What say we have our picnic over in the shade? I'm pretty hungry."

Izzy studied the secluded area, shaded from the sun. "Yes, let's." Turning to him, she flashed a smile. "I'm glad you thought of this. It's perfect."

No, Sam thought, taking in the sight of his bride. The only thing perfect in this setting was her. The simple walking skirt and blouse she wore formed to her body, curvier now that she'd been eating regularly. The way the pintucked bodice cupped her breasts reminded him of what treasures lay beneath the thin material. His body tightened, remembering how their delicate nubs tasted on his tongue.

Tearing his gaze away, Sam gripped the reins of the team and slowed the buckboard he'd borrowed from the Galleria. It took him an extra moment to squelch his desire. This wasn't the time or place to make love to his new bride. Right now he simply wanted to steal a few hours alone with her, maybe lay some groundwork for their first real intimacy.

Perhaps tonight, if she was ready.

Hell, I'm more than ready.

Climbing down, Sam came around to her side. Gripping her narrow waist, he delighted in the soft feel of her as she slid down his body until her feet touched the ground. Unable to resist, he planted a swift kiss on her lips. "Did I tell you how lovely you look today?"

"You might have, but feel free to say it again." She fluttered her lashes at him. "You can tell me anything, Just Sam."

He groaned. "You won't let me forget that, will you?"

"Probably not."

"Contrary miss." It felt good to forget his responsibilities for a while and indulge in teasing his wife. With a grin, Sam gathered up the quilt he'd swiped from one of the unused Galleria rooms and handed it to her, hefting the basket containing their lunch from beneath the seat.

Together, they spread out the colorful cotton beneath the tree and sat. Izzy tucked her legs under her skirt, affording him a brief flash of one ankle and slender, slippered foot. He'd have liked nothing better than to get more than a quick look, picturing her long, shapely legs . . .

He doused that train of thought. To distract himself, he gestured toward her deep green skirt. "One of your birthday gifts?"

"It is. Catherine told me her mother-by-marriage made it." Izzy raised her arm, revealing the unbuttoned and rolled up sleeve of her blouse. "She sewed my shirtwaist, too."

"Lucinda has a fine hand with a needle."

"And this hat from the milliners. I've never seen anything so lovely." Izzy picked up the beribboned, wide-brimmed boater. "Retta told me the lady who makes them is her aunt." She blinked up at him. "Everyone has been wonderful. They don't even know me and they're all so kind."

"Izzy, *you're* wonderful. Of course the folk around here would think well of you." Sam caught her left hand, where his ring glittered in the afternoon light. "Plus, they can see you make me happy."

She regarded him seriously. "Have I made you happy, Sam? Seems I haven't done anything at all." Her voice dropped to a low timbre. "Though you have already given me so much." She slid closer to him on the thick quilt, her skirt rustling as it twisted up along her legs. "What could I offer in return?"

Need clawing inside him, Sam swallowed hard and groped for the basket. If he didn't take some sort of mundane action—right this instant—he'd have her pinned to the ground and her petticoat bunched around her waist. Between denying himself the night before, and his longing for her now, it was all he could do not to snatch her up and take what she so innocently offered.

Their picnic spot was far enough out of town, he figured no one would bother them. Nobody would see if they—

Stop it. Izzy deserved more than a fast roll on a quilt under a tree. "Let's see what Dolores packed for us," he said, a bit too heartily, digging inside the basket.

"Sam—"

He focused on the contents of the basket instead of how appealing she looked sitting next to him in the dappled shade. "I'll bet she sent along chicken." He dug deeper. "She knows how much you love her chicken."

"Sam." She reached for his arm.

He jumped to his feet, tipping the basket and spilling some of its contents. "I can't find the jug of lemonade. I must've left it in the wagon."

Izzy rose to confront him, slamming her hands on her hips. "*Samuel Singleton.* What is the matter with you?"

Her annoyed frown made him want her even more. His lips twitched involuntarily.

"Nothing, I—oh, hell." He swept her into his arms, relishing the feel of her supple form against him. She embraced him in return.

Sam wanted her so badly he could barely string together an explanation that would make sense. With every hardship Izzy had already endured in her short life, he wanted to take things slow with her and make their first time special, treat her with the tenderness and respect she deserved.

Easing away, he gazed down at her. "Everything's fine. And last night . . . well, last night I wanted to make you feel good. Intimacy can be a fierce thing. I didn't want to scare you with my, er, lust."

Her eyes widened, perhaps with understanding. "You didn't scare me at all. You made me feel special and desired." She stroked his tense jaw. "I'm young but I'm not a girl barely out of my bloomers. And I won't break if you—"

"If I what?" He nibbled her ear, all his senses on fire for her. "If I touch you? Kiss you?" His throat tightened, picturing all he wanted to do to her. "Make love to you?"

"Yes to everything," she said on a sigh. Taking the initiative, she lifted on tiptoes to tentatively kiss him.

Sam responded instantly, deepening the kiss, groaning at the way she parted her lips and let him in, the way her tongue swept against his. Succumbing to the desire to bear her down to the quilt and provide them with the pleasure they both sought, he bent over her—

The bullet came from nowhere and hit the tree they stood next to, right where his head had been only seconds earlier.

Sam tumbled her to the ground, flinging himself over her. He curved his arms around her head. "Stay down, Izzy."

She tensed against him. "Was that a gun?"

"Yes," he hissed in her ear. "Someone shot at us."

Willy slammed into the parlor and headed straight for the liquor. Grabbing the first bottle in reach, he uncorked it and gulped, not bothering with a glass. The bourbon burned all the way down his throat.

A large hand descended on his shoulder and flipped him around. Unsteady, Willy managed to keep his feet. Dalton's beady eyes narrowed until only a slit of color remained.

"You failed," he snarled, shaking Willy hard. "I should have known better than to send a stupid boy to do a man's job."

"L-Let go." Willy struggled against the punishing grip. "You should've gone out there and taken the shot instead of me. She's *your* damned betrothed." He wrenched himself away, clutching the half-empty bottle, and staggered to the far end of the room. "I want the money you owe me." He sank onto a tufted ottoman and brought the bourbon to his lips.

"I don't pay for target practice on trees." Dalton brushed imaginary lint from his coat. "You'll get nothing from me."

Infuriated, Willy threw the bottle across the floor, uncaring of the spattered liquor and glass everywhere as it hit the corner of the hearth and exploded. "You promised me a reward for shooting Singleton—"

"I promised you money for killing him, not shearing off tree bark. Maybe this will teach you to do better next time."

"Next time? I'm not putting myself out for you again." Willy dragged himself to his feet, his boots crunching over splintered glass as he advanced on Dalton. "I hid for hours behind a trash heap, waiting for him to make a move, following him and my blasted sister out of town. I'm done. You want him dead, do it yourself."

His words were brave, even as he gave the older man a wide berth. Circling him warily, Willy headed for the stairs and his sitting room on the second floor where another full bottle awaited him.

Dalton's grating voice stopped him. "Brush up on your pathetic aim, boy. Next time we go hunting, I expect you to hit what you point at."

Chapter 17

Sam followed Joshua up the steps of Silver Cache's jailhouse to meet with Robert Blackwood about the incident with Izzy. Alerted by Abner Dale regarding an incoming telegram, they'd stopped by the coach station first before leaving Little Creede, and now had additional information he hoped would help in Maggie's investigation.

Entering the square building, they found the erstwhile sheriff tacking up wanted posters on the slat board. "Fresh faces courtesy of the Warden over at Territorial?" Joshua inquired, inspecting the sketches, a few rougher than others. "Maybe this time they'll actually remember to send me copies."

Robert pounded in a nail before turning, one thick brow raised. "Hello, boys. What brings you to my town?"

Sam tipped up the brim of his slouch and met Blackwood's questioning stare. "We had some trouble in Little Creede we need to speak to you about."

Blackwood crossed to his desk and settled himself. "Well, have a seat and let's hear it."

Sam dragged a chair from the front and straddled it.

Joshua remained standing. "Robert, we believe Willy McDougall, or possibly Reginald Dalton, shot at Sam and his wife yesterday."

Resurgent anger throbbed in Sam's veins. "I took Izzy on a picnic out near Surrey Pasture, under that cluster of pines where Vivian sometimes brings her class for their nature forays. Damned shot came out of nowhere and hit the tree right where we'd been standing. If I hadn't moved when I did, I wouldn't be talking to you right now." He dug into his shirt pocket, retrieving the spent bullet he'd pried out of the trunk, and tossed it on the desk. "It's small, like something Willy's .22 Short would use. I bet you'll find it matches."

Robert picked up the bullet and studied it thoroughly. "Even if it's the same model, it doesn't prove McDougall's the culprit."

"I realize that," Sam agreed. "It'll at least put him on notice he's under suspicion. Might stop him from trying again."

Scowling, Joshua edged forward. "We should head out to McDougall's. I have a few words for the man myself."

The door creaked and a tall, stocky man entered, wearing a deputy badge pinned to his checkered shirt. He tipped his Stetson in greeting to Sam and Joshua. "Gentlemen."

"Morning, Ray," Robert replied. "Boys, I'd like you to meet my deputy, Ray Bowman."

"Pleasure." Joshua clasped Ray's meaty paw for a hearty handshake. "I'm Joshua Lang. My deputy Ben Parsons mentioned you a time or two."

"All good, I hope." Ray's deep guffaw filled the room. "Ben and I go a long way back. He mentioned he worked for you now in Little Creede. Nice to finally meet you, Sheriff Lang."

"He sang your praises." Joshua gestured to Sam who'd risen to his feet. "Singleton here handles security at the Galleria in our town."

A broad smile split Ray's face, well-grooved laugh lines creasing his eyes as he shook Sam's hand. "I have yet to visit the establishment. Gotta save up my bettin' silver."

"Ray," Robert said, "can you run over to the saloon and fetch Willy McDougall? I saw him there during my rounds. We have a few questions for him."

"Sure, boss." Ray clomped to the door and left.

Robert sighed. "I've been doing some more digging into Reginald Dalton. The man's as bad an egg as it gets."

Sam's interest piqued. "What'd you learn?"

"Dalton and the McDougall men have been business partners on a lot of different projects over the years."

"What sort of projects?" Joshua inquired, rubbing his whiskered jaw.

"Maggie discovered the two were business associates in some shady but mostly legal gambling establishments before moving out West. She also learned William the Third has a nasty gambling problem, and he was barred from most Chicago gaming houses."

Joshua grunted thoughtfully. "So, McDougall's in debt to some dangerous people."

Sam straightened. "Sounds right. I had an old acquaintance do some digging for me. According to my contact, Izzy's father lost a sizable purse at faro gaming. I figure that's the reason the man's so intent on marrying his daughter off to Dalton, to settle a debt."

"Afraid it's more than that, Sam," Robert replied. "Maggie said your wife's mother received a large sum of money from her father when he passed. Additional information turned up her full name—Maureen O'Leary McDougall—and she receives a hefty, yearly disbursement from a Chicago law firm handling the estate. An incorruptible law firm, I hear. Old man O'Leary chose well."

"Interesting," Joshua mused aloud. "What happened after the mother disappeared?"

"They continued to disburse the funds. Until recently. The Chicago firm contacted Berger's office, requesting verification that McDougall's wife is alive before they'll release any more money."

Unable to stand still as his tension rose, Sam began pacing. "What happens to the trust fund if Missus Maureen dies?"

"If she's declared dead, the trust fund payments roll over to Izzy."

"All of it?" Joshua asked.

"Every. Last. Coin." Robert enunciated each word as his gaze landed on first Joshua, then Sam. "If this information bears out, it'd make your new bride a very wealthy woman. Maggie's office is working with a reliable source out of Chicago, and we hope to have a monetary figure soon."

Joshua glanced at Sam. "Wonder if Izzy knows?"

Sam shook his head. "I don't think so. And until we have some sort of evidence, we should keep this quiet. She's got enough on her shoulders right now. I don't want to burden her with anything more."

Robert added, "We should know within the week."

"How long does her father have to produce his wife?" Sam asked.

"Thirty days. He's got about fourteen left."

Sam ran his thumb across the underside brim of his slouch, a nervous habit he'd picked up from his riverboat days. "If true, in fourteen days they stand to lose their yearly disbursement and Izzy gets it all. Unless her mother turns up, alive and hopefully, well."

"Yep," Robert put in, "and if Maureen McDougall is declared deceased, then the payments stop. The race would be on to get Izzy married off, ensuring her inheritance falls into the hands of a husband of her father's choosing."

Joshua grunted in agreement. "Sounds like you'd best keep your head down and guard your pretty new bride, Singleton. Because McDougall and Dalton are desperate men."

"And there's nothing a desperate man won't do to get what he wants," Sam finished for him.

"Right. So, watch your back, and lock Izzy down for the next couple weeks until the threat's passed."

The door suddenly flew open and Ray shoved a struggling Willy inside.

Izzy finished up with the supper dishes and dried her hands on her apron. "Well, that's the last of them, Dolores. Is there anything else you need?"

"Naw, you go on now."

Taking off the soiled apron, she tossed it into the laundry bin. "Thank you. I'll see you in the morning."

"Night." Dolores cracked a wide smile. "I'm sure your young fella is looking for you by now."

Not bothering to tell her Sam had ridden over to Silver Cache to speak with the sheriff there, Izzy headed for the main salon. "You have a good evening, Dolores."

"Not as good as you're gonna have, I reckon." Her eyes twinkling, she produced an exaggerated sigh and fanned her face with her hand.

Izzy smiled, amused at the woman's antics. Her thoughts flashed back to the moment Sam surrendered to the desire that burned brightly between them—

Before they'd been shot at.

I'm not going to dwell on it.

She pushed open the door. "Goodnight, Dolores."

Too restless to retire for the evening, Izzy decided to explore the Galleria more thoroughly, since she hadn't a chance yet to see all the salons.

Reaching the main gaming area, she peeked inside, awed by the lavishness of the polished wood and felt-topped tables. Walls of burgundy velvet flocking proclaimed opulence everywhere she looked. Striped satin seating on the low chairs and scattered settees offered comfort and relaxation. Overhead, chandeliers dripped with faceted glass and delicate blown chimneys as fine as anything she'd ever seen.

The next two smaller parlors were equally as impressive, one set up for meals and the other meant for a gentleman's drinking pleasure. Both boasted the same elegant wall coverings and lush carpets. The faint hint of expensive cigars lingered in the air, probably left over from last week's tourney. Knight often closeted himself in his salons to indulge in a smoke and what he called a 'snort.' Sneezing at the smell, she backed out.

Noticing another rear saloon, she poked her head inside a half-open door, recognizing a private faro gaming room. Big money was won and lost at faro, her father's favorite form of gambling. Sighing, she shook off memories better left alone.

A grand piano, positioned near the far corner, gleamed in the low light of the kerosene sconces placed with military precision along each wall. The unexpected sight of it drew her like a bee to a flower. Entering the room, she dodged tables and random seating to reach the beautiful instrument.

"Oh," she murmured approvingly, "A Steinway."

She'd played piano from as far back as she could remember. An older upright in the lobby had tempted her on several occasions, with no opportunity to try it out due to the constant flow of gaming gents, coming and going. However, this glorious instrument . . . she couldn't resist.

Sweeping her skirts to the side, she took a seat on the bench. Pulse racing with excitement, she brought her hands up and played the scales to reintroduce herself to the keys.

Happiness bubbled up inside her, and she let her fingers dance softly across the ivory keys. Her body swayed slightly, the subtle drama of "Moonlight Sonata" rising in the air. Her mother had always loved "Beethoven's First Movement," and Izzy heard it so often she could play the entire piece by memory.

Reaching the end of the sonata, she sat quietly, filled with an inner peace as the last melodic note faded away.

Sam's voice suddenly carried across the room. "That was wonderful, Izzy."

Startled, she twisted around to find him in the doorway. Her pulse now raced for an entirely different reason. "Sam, when did you get back?"

"Just now. I went looking for you. Then I heard the music and had to follow it." He approached her with a look of determination. "And found me the sweetest woman performing one of my favorite compositions."

She rose to her feet as he crossed the room, until he stood directly in front of her with a bemused expression.

"You're full of surprises, Wife. I didn't know you played."

Izzy nodded inanely as her mind lost focus. Her body came alive with a myriad of sensations she now understood only her husband could satisfy. Yet she strove for some semblance of calm. "My mother taught me." At the fond memory, a smile curved her lips. "I played every day. Until—"

Her happiness rapidly evaporated, replaced by a piercing sadness.

Sam's brow furrowed. "Until what?"

"After my mother's disappearance, Father sold my piano."

Anger flashed across his face. "Your father's a horse's ass."

Izzy blinked, a laugh bubbling up from her throat at how her husband defended her. The growing affection she held for him unfolded deep inside, until her entire being brimmed with newfound joy and contentment.

Is this what love feels like?

"So quick to champion me, Mister Singleton," she managed, swallowing the last of her mirth.

"Always, Missus Singleton." Clasping her wrist, he tugged her into his arms. "As your husband, it's my duty to stand with you, even against your own family."

His gaze dropped to her mouth. Izzy moistened her lips, aching for more of his touch, the unfamiliar tingling in her limbs strengthening when he lowered his head to kiss her.

His mouth lingered, soft and gentle, his tongue flicking across the seam of her lips until they parted for him. As she clutched the back of his shirt, he tilted her head to take the kiss deeper.

One arm tightening around her waist, he lifted her until her toes barely touched the floor. Something thick and hard pushed intimately against her, its heat permeating through her skirts. She'd seen enough in the stockyards to understand what that hardness represented.

He kissed her with such rising passion, she lost track of place and time. Everything centered on this one moment, with this man, her husband. She craved Sam in ways she still didn't quite understand, her body growing pliant, lost to the feel of him. The taste of him. The way his masculine scent cocooned her in comfort and promise.

All too soon, he pulled away. Izzy's whimper of protest was met with an answering groan.

She slowly opened her eyes.

The fire in Sam's gaze, a scant inch away, scorched her. She licked his flavor from her lips, trembling with need. "Why'd you stop?"

"Because when I make love to you for the first time, it won't be in one of the Galleria's salons."

"Oh." How could she have forgotten where they were? Izzy sent a panicked glance around, relieved they were still alone.

He released her, entwining their fingers. "Let's go." He pulled her toward the door.

Izzy hurried to keep up with his long strides. "Where are we going?"

"To our suite," came the husky reply.

She glanced outside. The sun had yet to set for the evening, casting a golden glow over the town. "It's not dark yet."

"We wouldn't be sleeping, Izzy."

"Oh," she repeated like an idiot as his reasoning dawned on her.

He paused at the foot of the grand staircase. "If you don't want this, tell me now and we can take a leisurely stroll outside."

"No." She wanted nothing more than to spend the night in this man's arms.

He nuzzled a kiss over her lips, then reversed course toward the exit. "A walk it is."

Izzy dug in her heels, causing him to stop and send her a questioning glance. "No. That's not what I meant. I mean—no, I don't want to go for a walk . . ." Her voice trailed off.

"Thank God." He swept her into his arms, taking the stairs two and three at a time.

Izzy clutched at his shoulders, strangely excited by his behavior. "Sam, you should put me down."

"Nope."

Seconds later, Sam set her on the floor in front of their suite and unlocked the door, swinging it wide.

"After you, sweet Izzy." The teasing glint in his dark eyes made them glow.

Suddenly shy, Izzy couldn't hold his gaze. As soon as she crossed the threshold the door clicked shut, and Sam's arms came around her. His soft kisses tickled her neck as he unfastened her gown, not fumbling with the thin whalebone buttons the way she often did. "Is this all right?"

Her stomach swirled with anticipation. Her heart thumped so hard and fast, surely Sam could hear it. Moisture pooled between her legs, a reminder of the aching desire she'd felt once already at his hands.

As the back of her gown parted, the open window's breeze cooled her heated skin, followed by the allure of Sam's lips trailing over her nape above her linen chemise.

"You're softer than satin," he murmured as he pushed the sprigged cotton off her shoulders, where it caught at her elbows. When his lips soothed over a patch of raised scarring that retained a twinge of discomfort, she trembled at his tenderness, at how carefully he touched her.

He toyed with the straps of her chemise, and Izzy was fiercely glad she'd left off her corset as a concession to working in the hot kitchen earlier. With less clothing to bother with, Sam soon had her bared to the waist.

Peppering her neck and shoulders with kisses, he brought his hands around to cup her breasts. Loving how his large palms enveloped her as she relaxed against him, she sighed in approval when he squeezed her sensitive mounds, then tweaked the tips. Pleasure zipped through her, lodging deep within her and eliciting a throaty moan.

Sam's hands fell away. Before she could protest, he scooped her up and strode over to deposit her on their bed. Reclining on the soft coverlet, watching him watch her, increased her excitement. Her breathing grew erratic. His gaze locked on her breasts, their buds taut and peaked.

A tremor of yearning overwhelmed her.

Sam rested one knee on the bed. "I'm going to remove your gown, Izzy." Without waiting for a response, he tugged the loose fabric at her waist—her pantalets, too—pulling everything over her hips and down her legs. The thin batiste caught on her slippers, and he removed them as well, leaving her naked as the day she was born.

Besides her mother, no one had ever seen her unclothed. Under her husband's intense regard, she instinctively brought her hands up to cover herself, her innate modesty battling with the unfurling desire inside her.

Only approval shone in his eyes as he stripped off his shirt and unbuckled his holster. Setting them both on the chair next to him, he kicked off his boots. Through it all his eyes never left hers.

How could she know a man's gaze held so much emotion and caring?

Because the only men you have ever known are bounders and cads.

Not this one, standing over her, still wearing his trousers as if understanding she might not be ready for him to completely disrobe.

Sam caught hold of her hands and pulled them away from her attempt to hide. He took her in from tangled hair to fidgeting toes, a thoroughly slow perusal. "I've never seen such perfection."

The sincerity in his voice eased some of her bashfulness. Izzy's tentative smile seemed to be the encouragement he needed as he came down over her, pressing her into the mattress. The feel of his skin against hers banished the rest of her shyness and uncertainty.

She wound her arms around his neck as he took her mouth in a passionate kiss. All the while his hands ran over her, gentle and exploring, making her moan, until he finally stroked the spot where she hungered for his touch the most.

Her cry of delight echoed off the walls. Izzy let go of any remaining hesitation as she allowed herself to enjoy Sam's large, gentle hands; those wonderful lips . . .

Murmuring words of encouragement, he bathed her in ardent kisses while continuing to do wicked things to her body. His tender touch drove her pleasure higher and higher, until she thought she'd die if he didn't take her over the edge again.

Eyes squeezed tightly shut, she lifted her hips, silently begging him to finish what he'd begun, or she'd lose her mind.

"Hold tight to me, honey." He suddenly slid down her body.

Her eyes popped open in surprise, peering down in time to see him bury his head between her legs. Scandalized, she instinctively clamped them around his head. Parting her lips to tell him to stop, she whimpered instead as he slid two fingers inside her.

Then she felt his tongue flick against a particularly sensitive spot once, twice.

"Ohmygod," she cried out, her legs falling open as she grasped at his hair to hold him more firmly against her. "Sam—"

Unable to form another coherent word, her quivering body clamped down tight on his fingers. Sucking her gently, his dark groan against her quivering flesh was enough to catapult her over the precipice into an explosion of pure bliss she'd never dreamed possible.

Lost in sensation, she was vaguely aware of Sam standing next to the bed, yanking off his trousers, then returning to ease her legs wider.

With one sharp thrust, he breached her maidenhood, the sting only lasting a second before he sent her straight to heaven.

Chapter 18

Izzy's blushing cheeks and shy glances had set the tone for the day, and Sam was grateful for the extra time with her. Still in their nightclothes, they sat across from each other at the marble-topped table in their suite, enjoying the tea Dolores had provided for them. After assuring him Izzy wasn't needed until suppertime, the cook had shooed Sam out of the kitchen with the tea tray.

Even as he pondered the best way to tell Izzy about the confrontation he'd had at the Silver Cache jail with her brother, his body tightened, remembering how last night he'd been otherwise occupied, drowning in the passion between them that'd resulted in such a sweet consummation.

He couldn't wait any longer. She needed to understand the threat her family still posed. Not yet willing to share what he'd learned about her mother for fear of ruining any lingering hope she might still be clinging to, he could at least stress the importance of laying low until more evidence was uncovered. Draining the last of the lukewarm tea, he set down the cup.

"C'mere." Sam tugged her to her feet and led her to the flowered chaise beneath the parlor window. She settled next to him with a soft sigh, resting her head on his shoulder. The quiet in the sunlit room added to Sam's contentment—something he was loath to shatter with talk of the 'Terrible Trio,' as he'd started dubbing them.

It had to be done. He refused to leave her in the dark on something affecting her so directly. "Izzy, I wanted to talk with you about my trip yesterday to Silver Cache to see Sheriff Blackwood."

"I figured it had something to do with my pathetic excuse of a family."

"It does. Robert's wife, Maggie, heard a few things since she apprentices with Attorney Berger. Probably nothing you didn't already know. Your father's gambling woes seem to have driven his actions over the years."

She snuggled into him. "For as far back as I can remember, Father would come home late at night smelling of whiskey and cigars. He'd start arguments with my mother who for the most part was a calm soul. She tried to shield me from their confrontations, but I often heard them.”

“I’m sorry, honey.” Sam tightened his arms around her, wishing he could wipe away the memories as well as the pain.

“Why does everything seem to begin and end with the drive for money?” Izzy asked sadly. “In Chicago we had enough to run a household, put food on the table.” She suddenly straightened and faced him on the wide cushion. Anger now tightened her beautiful features. “Father gambled something fierce, and often hit my mother when she fought with him about it.”

Sam’s gut clenched at the thought of Maureen McDougall becoming a receptacle for her husband’s violence. Rubbing Izzy’s nape soothingly, he strove for temperance. “Would you say your father lost more at gambling than he won?” he finally asked.

“I think so.”

He probed carefully, unsure of how much his young wife actually knew about her family’s circumstances. “It’s the man’s duty to see to the finances of the family. Your father might have dabbled in the higher stakes games.”

“Father favored faro more than any other game, even poker.” She paused for a moment. “Sometimes the men he played with would follow him home after a game. Mother never liked it when they did. She would come up to my room and lock the door. She’d stay with me all night.” Izzy raised her head to look at Sam. “When I got older and we moved to Colorado, I realized Mother had protected us from any of Father’s drunken cronies who might’ve become too rowdy. After we settled in Silver Cache and Mother . . . disappeared,” she whispered painfully, “that’s when Reginald Dalton visited for the first time and Father let him stay at our house. I remembered my mother’s caution and made sure to lock my door.”

“Christ.” The curse exploded from Sam’s throat. “Tell me Dalton didn’t lay a hand on you.”

“He didn’t.” Her cheeks blanched but her voice held firm. “In Chicago I was too young. By the time we settled in Silver Cache I was smart enough to understand he would someday have the right, if Father trapped me into marriage with him.” A shudder rippled over her. “I couldn’t allow that to happen.”

Forcing down his dark emotions, Sam rubbed his wife's shoulders soothingly until she relaxed. From what he'd learned at the Silver Cache jail, Izzy's very existence became a threat to her criminal, money-grubbing menfolk unless they found her a suitable husband who'd control her wealth as well as strike some sort of deal to keep them in funds.

Such as Reginald Dalton.

Remembering the way her eyes had glowed first thing this morning from being well-satisfied last night, still innocent despite all they'd done, he bent to kiss her soft lips.

Without additional proof, he couldn't bear to disillusion her further. Until he uncovered more, he'd keep her safe.

In the lamplit parlor, shadows cast Reginald Dalton's expression into forbidding lines. "Craven idiot. You confessed everything to the sheriff."

Willy sprawled on the floor, rubbing his jaw.

Should've stayed in my room.

But hunger had driven him downstairs in hopes of a decent meal. Instead he'd found himself on the receiving end of punishing knuckles.

He glared hatefully up at the older man. "Next time you swing a fist, I'm gonna kill you."

"Unlikely." Dalton's boot stomped hard on Willy's knee. He cried out in pain as the bastard stared him down. Willy looked away, struggling not to holler again.

"I didn't tell them anything," he protested, trying to dislodge the heel pushing against his abused limb.

"Only because I interrupted Sheriff Blackwood, mid-interrogation, with my inspired grass fire." Dalton studied his nails as if bored. He continued to grind his boot, forcing a squeal from Willy's throat. "You can thank me later for dropping that lit matchstick, by the way."

Willy clamped his lips shut, not about to thank him for anything.

"Get your foot off my boy," his father barked. By the way he stumbled across the room, Willy guessed Father had already quaffed his weight in liquor. Swaying, he came to a stop in front of Dalton, bloodshot eyes blinking as he tried and failed to appear intimidating. "He didn't tell Blackwood anything."

"How would you know, old man?" Dalton snarled. "You were too busy filling your belly with the whiskey my generosity provides."

When he eased off enough for Willy to free his leg, he scuttled away awkwardly, ending up between the sofa and a faded ottoman. Unable to gain his feet, he glowered at the dapper Reginald, wishing he could pull his pistol and shoot the sumbitch dead. "I kept my mouth shut. Never said a thing. When Blackwood ran out of the jail, the others had no reason to hold me any longer, and they knew it."

Not for anything would he admit to his bowel-loosening fear when Sheriff Lang threatened him. Empty threats, because as long as Willy remained in Silver Cache, he fell under town jurisdiction and Lang had no proof elsewhere. Refusing to dirty his hands further in Little Creede could assure his safety. He'd heard enough rumors about Territorial Prison to know he never wanted to end up in that hellhole.

Willy managed to lever himself onto the ottoman, rubbing his knee and wincing, while Dalton strolled to the side credenza and selected one of the delicate cup-and-saucer sets Isadora had favored for her tea. Willy eyed him warily, half-expecting the pompous ass to lob the expensive china at him. The older man merely poured the steaming brew from a matching teapot and lifted the cup to his mouth, his little finger outthrust as if he were some royal nob.

Willy looked on in disgust.

Dalton drained the tea, then chucked the cup and saucer across the room, narrowly missing Father's head. One after the other hit the fireplace andirons, the fragile china shattering into pieces, flying everywhere.

"Here, now," the old man blustered. "That was part of a set I gifted to my wife upon our wedding—"

Dalton sneered. "Bought with her money, no doubt. Did you care about the things you gave the enchanting Maureen, the night you strangled her?" he taunted in a soft, deadly voice. "I'm prepared to overlook what I know of the more unsavory details of your wife's demise, William. You'd do well to remember that."

"I'm well aware of what you promised and what I agreed upon, Reginald." Willy's father sagged where he stood, the tremble in his hands obvious as he wrung them. "I merely wanted to point out these items have been designated as a dowry and will pass to you through Isadora."

"As if that matters," Willy retorted in derision.

"For once, your imbecile offspring is correct." Dalton picked a speck of lint from his cuff. His eyes, when he fixed them on Willy's father, held pure frost. "Broken or whole, Isadora and her *items* will belong to me. I anticipate a very satisfying wedding night, once she has returned to the bosom of her loving family and her widowhood verified." He licked his lips and showed his teeth in a biting smile.

Willy allowed himself a brief shudder on his sister's behalf, telling himself it wasn't any of his business what Reginald Dalton did to Isadora once he married her. He rubbed his sore knee harder. "Get her yourself, then."

"If you want my continued generosity, boy, you'll do as I say," came the low, icy response. "Unless you'd prefer to scrabble for food and gambling vouchers on your own."

As Dalton's words sank in, Willy's bravado shrank. Caught, he had no choice but to risk his own life and retrieve his sister, even if it meant stealing into a town where his hide wasn't worth cow flop. He told himself it only mattered what generous settlement Dalton would settle on him and his father, enough to allow them a comfortable existence with extra gaming funds.

He promised us and he won't rescind it, Willy thought, rallying his confidence.

Wasn't much else he could do.

He started to rise from the low ottoman, when a fist waved in front of him. Willy drew back, blinking in confusion, his attention caught by the lethal-looking shard of broken saucer Dalton held mere inches away. "What the—"

Piercing, fiery agony slashed across his cheek from ear to jaw. Screaming in pain, Willy flailed backward over the ottoman and landed on his head. When he probed the injured area, his palm came away covered with blood. "You cut me!"

Brandishing the sharp, red-tipped weapon, Dalton snarled, "Threaten my life again, and I'll slit you from ear to ear."

Pleasantly full, Izzy folded her hands in her lap and sat quietly next to Sam, occasionally glancing around the main parlor of the Miner Stage House. With its subtly striped wallpaper and comfortable seating, vases of wildflowers dotting the glossy surfaces of the tables scattered about, the room offered a welcoming respite.

They'd enjoyed a midday meal of roast hare and squash, followed by a thick slice of chess pie so reminiscent of her mother's recipe, Izzy almost cried. An invitation of peach nectar and coffee in the parlor offered a chance for her to calm herself. By the time Joshua, then Lucinda Blackwood joined them, Izzy felt better.

Lucinda smiled warmly, and Izzy marveled anew at how the vibrant woman before her claimed seven grandchildren already. Uncommonly lovely, she personified elegance from the top of her upswept, burnished curls, to the tips of her pretty green slippers matching her deep emerald gown. Sparkling amber eyes, offset by thick dark lashes, held a wealth of maturity as well as humor.

Joshua Lang sat on the sofa with his boots propped on a low table, the picture of relaxation next to his mother-by-marriage. Until she poked him in the stomach and admonished, "Sit up straight, son."

"Yes, ma'am." He hastily complied and dropped both feet to the floor, shoving long brown hair out of his eyes. He winked at Izzy. "She gets after me," he explained, earning him an affectionate cuff upside the head. He rubbed his ear in reaction, aiming a smile at Lucinda which she returned.

Sam snorted as Izzy suppressed the urge to giggle. More and more, she found herself fascinated by the way the extended Carter family treated each other, a combination of love, trust, and abiding loyalty so different from her own current miseries.

"Now," Lucinda began, regarding Sam expectantly, "Joshua says you have some questions regarding the law in Bolster."

"I do, Missus Lucinda. Do you think the Marshall in your hometown would be willing to share information on the criminal element in the general Chicago vicinity?"

Both of Lucinda's perfectly shaped eyebrows arched. "You expect Marshall Fulsome knows enough about Chicago's underbelly to offer names, places, and deeds?" She regarded Joshua. "You might have warned me, Sheriff."

"Ma, this is important. Izzy could be in danger from her own family unless we can uncover what sort of underhanded dealings they'd have gotten involved in." Joshua leaned forward, elbows propped on his knees, and favored Izzy with a somber look. "We figured you had no idea your menfolk were breaking the law in Chicago. Am I right?"

Izzy clutched Sam's arm, finding comfort in his warmth. After what she'd dealt with in Silver Cache, her youthful ignorance growing up in Chicago felt shameful. "I spent most of my time with my mother, back then. Father had an office where he worked long hours. I never knew he dabbled in law until we moved to Silver Cache and he spoke of hanging a shingle on Main Street."

"Is it possible he presented himself as an attorney during those years in Chicago?" Joshua urged. "There might be something on city record."

"I can't say for sure. I was so young and sheltered." Izzy turned to Sam who immediately slipped an arm around her. "I'm not much help, am I?"

"We'll figure it out." He rose, bringing Izzy up with him. "Missus Lucinda, if you think the Bolster law might be of assistance, we'll telegraph their office today."

"Direct it to Marshall Herbert Fulsome and mention my name. I believe he'll be willing to help."

Sunset dusted the shadows outside the kitchen windows, opened wide to take advantage of the breeze. Dolores baked on Sunday, the wood oven coals kept stoked all morning. Wiping her perspiring forehead on her sleeve, Izzy crossed to the center counter where a stack of dirty dishes still remained.

Knight's habit of serving a 'donation only' Sunday supper drew folks in town and sometimes beyond, paying for their meal with everything from raw silver ore to eggs. Last week, Ike Barnes's gift of a butchered cow was met with eternal gratitude from Dolores. The Galleria never turned anyone away, the extra meal especially welcome since Catherine closed the Stage House dining after Sunday luncheon, reopening her kitchen again on Monday morning.

Today's menu at the Galleria included river trout with creamed milkweed, and fresh peas from Trudy Parsons' garden. If Izzy hadn't been so stuffed from earlier, she'd have loved some trout, a favorite of hers.

Knuckling the small of her back, she grimaced at the dampness there, and loosened her apron ties. More dishes awaited. A deep pan of water simmered on the stove, sending steam into the air, ready to scald the soapy plates and cups. While she scrubbed and scraped, Izzy let her mind wander to what awaited her once she went upstairs for the night. As she stood at the sink, up to her elbows in the dish tub, the image of Sam, bare-chested and hard-muscled, nearly brought her to her knees.

"Oh, my." She clutched the rim of the metal pan to steady herself. Part of her wanted to hide from the passion of their marriage bed, of the wanton pleasures she found in his embrace. The rest of her longed to forget her duties and fly up the back stairs, straight into his arms.

My husband.

A noise at the window roused her from her dreaming state. Izzy frowned, squinting at the darkening gloom past the drawn-back curtains. Seeing nothing, she returned to her soaking plates and scrub brush. Another scratch, this time at the door, made her wonder if a hungry cat might be outside, searching for food.

Abandoning the washing-up, she crossed to the slop pail Dolores kept for the hogs penned in the back of the property line near the stables. Surely the trout scraps hadn't been taken outside yet. A nice sized head might be just the thing for a ravenous stray.

The door burst open and banged loudly against the wall.

Izzy instinctively grabbed a knife from the carving block next to the stove and spun, coming eye to eye with her brother. Without hesitation she brought up the weapon. "Stay back and leave the way you came."

"Or what? You'd stick your own flesh and blood?" Willy stood cockily, arms loose at his sides. But his eyes showed his nervousness, one of them bruised and twitching. The left side of his face sported a long, shallow cut. He advanced unsteadily, favoring one leg. "Drop the knife, you're leaving with me."

Izzy couldn't drum up much sympathy for her older sibling. She firmed her grip on the knife and strove to hold it steady, locking her knees to keep them from shaking. "I'm not going anywhere with you. Get out of here before I scream for Sam."

Willy circled her, his limp more pronounced. A sluggish drop of blood pooled from the deepest part of his wound, dripping from his jaw onto his dirty shirt collar. Despite his injuries, Izzy kept him square in her sights, refusing to let him maneuver around her or try coming up from behind. Her brother could move damned fast when he wanted to, bad leg or not.

"I'm not leaving without you, Isadora." His voice dropped to a cajoling note. "You don't belong here." He inched closer. Izzy jerked back, her spine slamming into the wall where Dolores stored bins of oats and dried beans.

A sly smile transformed his damaged features into something twisted and ugly. "Gotcha," he crowed, snagging the hem of her apron and yanking. It came off in his fist as Izzy spun from the wall and made a break for the pantry, intending to barricade herself inside.

As she opened her mouth to scream, the cocking of a rifle froze them both in place. "Leave her alone," an angry female voice snapped from the door leading into the main salon.

Lowering the knife, Izzy breathed out a sigh of relief. *Thank goodness, Dolores and her shotgun.* She sidled along the pantry wall as Willy backed toward the doorway which still stood open, letting in moths attracted to the lit interior.

"I'm going, don't shoot. Stupid old hag," he flung at Dolores, limping to the threshold.

When she aimed the rifle dead center of his back, Izzy shook her head. Criminal or not, he was still her flesh and blood. "Let him go, Dolores."

"This ain't the end of it, sister," Willy growled. Turning at the back stoop, he yelled, "Ask your husband about how he married you for the fortune our miserly grandfather left you."

He disappeared from sight, his parting accusation rendering Izzy speechless.

Grandfather? A fortune? She whirled, almost tripping over her own feet, blinking at Dolores who'd lowered the rifle and uncocked it. "I—thank you, Dolores."

"You'd better go get Sam," the older woman urged, propping the rifle against the wall outside the salon entrance.

"Sam," Izzy echoed, sorting through implications, hating the mistrust they stirred up. "Yes, I think I should."

Chapter 19

After a hasty breakfast, fraught with tension, in their suite, Sam opened the door of the Galleria, allowing Izzy to exit. She passed him without so much as a word or glance, her stiff posture indicating her continued displeasure with him. Wearily, he rubbed the back of his neck and followed her out. The heat, already blasting from the early morning sun, indicated it'd be a hot day.

He'd made a mistake, withholding the information about her inheritance. Clearly she'd been hurt by the thought he'd only married her for the money she'd soon receive. No matter how hard he'd tried to convince her otherwise the prior evening, she'd closed off her mind and emotions, crawling into bed and turning her back to him.

Lying next to her, the sound of her tears had broken Sam's heart. Only after she'd worn herself out and fallen into a restless sleep had he gathered her close, gently stroking her hair until the stiffness in her body eased and she'd slept more peacefully. It'd been late into the night before Sam finally drifted off himself.

With a jaw-cracking yawn, he hurried to catch up to her as she approached the wagon. She'd asked him to take her out to Retta's today so she could lend a hand and visit. Some of the women had been taking turns cooking meals and helping out with the Carter brood since the birth of newborn Quinn. Vivian had been spending most of her time there, so he figured this was Izzy's way to avoid him for a while.

Though he didn't like it, he understood her mistrust, after the way she'd been treated by her own family. In her mind, he'd betrayed her in the worst way, and it'd take him time to repair the damage. Hopefully, Catherine and Vivian would come to his defense and pave the way for a quicker reconciliation with his charmingly delightful wife. Harrison and Elby would see to their safety, while Sam assisted Joshua in tracking down Willy to throw him in jail.

"Let me help you up." Sam gripped her slender waist and lifted her up onto the seat.

They traveled for a good half hour, her continued silence deafening, until he couldn't stand it any longer. "Are you ever going to speak to me again?" She didn't answer, studying the landscape as if it were the most important thing in the world. "Izzy, you have to know I didn't marry you for your inheritance."

Immediately he regretted his ill-tempered tone, but damn it, her attitude frustrated him. After their nights of passion, how could she think so little of him? He'd sheltered and cherished her since the moment he'd discovered her in the pantry, dirty, hungry, and scared.

When she furtively blotted away a tear, Sam's anger faded. He fisted the reins tightly, lowering his head in self-loathing. How could he have bungled things so badly?

She touched his arm and he met her sad gaze as she managed a tentative, "I'm trying to understand, Samuel."

He flinched at the more formal usage of his name. Hadn't they already disposed of such awkwardness?

Her hand dropped back into her lap. "Besides my mother, no one has ever cared about me or my feelings."

"Izzy—"

She shook her head vigorously. "No, let me finish."

A declaration, of how much he cared for her, poised on the tip of his tongue. Seeing how she wasn't yet ready to hear it, he clamped his lips tight.

Her soft sniffle felt like a kick to the gut.

"In my heart," she began, "I do believe you. I know you are a good man, Sam."

The tension in his shoulders eased some, until she added, "My head tells me to be cautious."

"I married you to keep you safe from your vile family," he ground out, unable to hold back his displeasure.

Shut your mouth, Singleton, he told himself, *you're only making things worse.* Izzy needed time to work through her emotions. She'd arrive at the right conclusions about their marriage. He should have faith and be patient with her.

"I'm sorry," she said in obvious distress. "I just need some time to sort this out for myself."

"I—" Sam started in response, when something shiny flashed off in the distance. Instinctively, he dropped the reins and shoved her down as his other hand went for his Colt.

A shot rang out.

Izzy screamed.

Sharp pain burst through Sam's head. The seat slats bit into his spine as the force of a bullet knocked him back.

"Sam," Izzy cried, scrambling to where he slumped against the seat, unresponsive, his head matted with blood. "Oh my God, Sam!"

Gripping his shirt with both hands, she tugged him into her arms. He flopped against her shoulder. Streams of blood poured from the top of his head, dripping onto her bodice. The pungent odor of iron, sweat, and dust made her stomach lurch as she fought nausea.

"No," she moaned. Glancing around frantically, she squinted against the bright sun to see a rider cantering across the prairie from a scattering of tall scrub in the distance.

Is that Willy?

Had her brother shot Sam? Possibly killed him?

For the barest of a second, she contemplated grabbing the reins and trying to flee. In a heavy wagon she'd never be able to outrun a single rider. "Sam," she sobbed, unable to stem her growing hysteria. "Please, please wake up!"

Hearing pounding hooves, Izzy dove for the floor of the buckboard where Sam's gun had fallen from his grip. She'd die protecting him. Grabbing up the Colt, Izzy spun around to confront Willy.

The pistol, slippery from Sam's blood, slid from her fingers and fell to the ground.

Before she could jump from the wagon and retrieve it, Reginald Dalton shoved a rifle at her. "Don't move, Isadora."

If Reginald suspected even for an instant that Sam might still be alive, he'd shoot again. Thinking fast, Izzy sidled carefully, shielding her husband from view, forcing her enemy to concentrate on her.

"You killed him," she spat, hoping he'd think Sam was already dead, and desperately praying he wasn't.

"No, your father killed him."

"What are you talking about?"

With a foul sneer Reginald twisted in the saddle and yanked at a rope holding a lumpy blanket draped across his horse's hindquarters.

As it loosened, the blanket fell to the ground, disgorging its ghastly contents.

Her father's corpse rolled once, settling in a heap, half his head blown off. A scream pierced the air, and it took a moment for Izzy to realize the sound came from her.

Reginald's burst of raucous laughter echoed all around her in the sudden stillness, as if even the animals sensed danger. She sucked in a harsh breath, gagging at the horror her eyes couldn't unsee.

Shedding tears for a father who'd never shown her any kindness, Izzy met Reginald's hard stare. "Why?" she begged.

"I have a document remanding you to your father's custody until this so-called marriage can be annulled."

Shock assailed her. "Who would sign such a thing?"

"I have friends in positions of influence, sweetheart. Not that it matters now, since your *husband*"—he spat the word—"is dead."

A wave of grief pummeled her. She didn't dare check on Sam, for fear of drawing attention to him.

Reginald's smile held all the evilness of the world. "When dear old William and I reached the outskirts of Little Creede, we spotted the wagon. I couldn't miss the opportunity to get rid of your father as I always intended." His dismissive gaze swept over her. "And make you a widow at the same time."

He swung down from the black stallion. In three long strides he reached the wagon. Izzy reared back but couldn't escape his punishing grip. With a hard jerk he sent her sprawling. She landed on her stomach near his horse with a pain-filled cry, tearing her skirts, her elbows and knees scraped. The animal reared up in alarm, its massive hooves barely missing her head as she rolled to one side.

He loomed over her threateningly. "You *will* be my wife, Isadora."

"*Never*," she grated, scrambling to her feet. "I'd die first."

"Oh, you may die." He grabbed for her wrist, grinding her fragile bones together and forcing a whimper from her throat. Dragging her toward Sam's Colt, he plucked it from the dirt. "*After* I get what I want, of course. You in my bed and your money in my bank."

Raising the gun, he aimed and shot her father in what was left of his head, the sharp report reverberating in Izzy's ears. Blackness pooled at the edges of her vision, and she wobbled on her feet, sobbing.

"Do stop your caterwauling." He wrenched her toward the wagon. "When I'm through with you, if you still want to end your life, I'll provide you with whatever tools you need."

Izzy pulled against him, to no avail. "You're insane. You'll hang for murder."

"No, dear girl. Samuel Singleton murdered William. When we showed him this perfectly legal document, he shot your father, then turned his gun on me." Reginald's grip tightened unbearably, pulling her harder as they reached the wagon and he tossed the Colt on the floorboards. "I had to shoot him first. It was self-defense." The tone of his voice held the arrogance of the wealthy.

"I'll tell everyone what you've done—"

"Who'd believe a weak-minded, unstable woman's rantings?" he scoffed, dragging her over a thistle bush. Izzy bit back a cry as thorns caught on her ankles.

Desperate for a glimpse of Sam, she swiveled at the same moment the black stallion whinnied loudly, stomping his hooves. Her eyes locked on a tooled leather bag buckled to the back of the saddle—and the slatted knife sheath attached to its flap.

The sheath contained a wicked looking Bowie.

If she got hold of it, maybe she could stab Reginald—

Or herself.

I'd rather die here with Sam than go anywhere with this despicable man.

As she agonized over how to get her hands on the weapon, the horse abruptly sidestepped. Cursing, Reginald released her wrist to catch its bridle, providing her the only chance she'd get at escape.

Lifting her skirts, she darted for the saddlebag and whipped the knife from its sheath. Spinning clumsily, she slashed at Reginald, aiming for his heart, slicing into his upper arm instead.

"Stupid bitch! You'll pay for that." He slammed his uninjured arm into her back, sending her flying.

The side of her head hit the ground as his fist filled her blurred vision.

Then everything went black.

Izzy awoke with the worst headache, stiff and aching. She groaned, her stomach churning and bouncing. Her eyes popped open.

She sat upon a galloping horse, the air stifling as the sun hung in the sky overhead.

A hard body pressed against her back, and like a curtain being drawn, she remembered what happened.

Sam. A silent sob shook her at the thought her kindhearted husband might be dead because of her. If she'd never come into his life, he'd still be alive. Even if he had survived the first bullet, had Reginald shot him again after she'd fainted? The guilt and remorse were crushing.

Reginald's arms tightened around her like bands of steel, pinning her in place.

"So, you're finally awake." His hateful comment burned against her ear.

She jerked, trying to insert a modicum of distance between them. Pain made her whimper aloud. She hurt everywhere, as if someone had pummeled her from head to toe.

Reginald laughed darkly. "My foot might have slipped a time or two after you knocked yourself out when you fell."

"You *shoved* me to the ground." Knowing he'd kicked her while she lay, unconscious and helpless, only reinforced the fact he was a monster.

"I'd have liked to damage you further. Thanks to your hamfisted attempt with my hunting knife, I'm going to need stitches." He squeezed her until she gasped for air. "I should have slit your dainty little throat. Except I need you alive for a bit longer."

"Where are you taking me?"

"None of your concern."

She could taste blood on her lips, vaguely recalling Reginald's fist swinging toward her face. *Sam's far braver than I've ever been.* He could survive more than a bullet; she had to hang on to her hope. The thought of him bleeding from a head wound swam in her mind, breaking her wide open again. Ruthlessly she squashed the image.

Her husband was too good and honorable to die by this horrid man's hands.

I have to believe he still lives and will find me.

Studying the area as they rode, Izzy didn't recognize anything. "Where are we?" Her repeat question earned her a slap to the back of her head, nearly toppling her from the horse.

"I said it's none of your concern. All you need to know about is our wedding, tomorrow." Reginald spoke calmly as if he discussed the weather instead of the ruination of her life.

"I'll never let you touch me." She struggled to break free from his hold, causing herself more agony as her stiff limbs cramped.

He retaliated by biting her earlobe. "Stop, or I'll let you fall on your head. Think how much it would hurt."

"I'd welcome breaking my neck or getting stomped from your horse." Izzy kept wriggling, her strength waning though she redoubled her efforts to free herself. "I vow, you won't get away with this heinous crime."

Her singular regret, that her last memory with Sam would be of them arguing, simply wrenched her heart. Why hadn't she trusted his word? He'd never have betrayed her.

"Heinous crime, eh? Oh, I'll succeed quite well, sweetheart. There's a judge close by here, an old acquaintance of mine from Chicago." Reginald's voice turned meaner. "He'll marry us, all nice and legal. And on our wedding night, the payment I'll extract from your not-so-virginal body will make you scream. You'll pay too, for cutting me and for allowing another man to touch you."

Hatred for this awful man boiled deep inside her. If she managed to get her hands on a gun, she'd shoot Reginald Dalton dead without one ounce of remorse. Pushing aside her grief, Izzy remained alert as they rode in silence, desperately searching for a way to escape.

A ranch house finally came into view. Two large men strode outside onto a wide-planked porch, their hard-looking appearance filling her with fear. Their facial similarities indicated they were probably related. The only remarkable difference was a jagged scar across one man's face.

"Well, I'll be, if it ain't Reggie Dalton." The scarred man snorted. "What the hell brings you all the way out here?"

The other man leered at Izzy, dashing any hopes of their help for escape. "Who's your plaything, Dalton?"

Reginald muttered, "The Shaw brothers would just as soon shoot you as molest you. Keep your mouth shut and I might not give you to them." He pushed her off the horse, dumping her on the ground. Her shaky legs collapsed beneath her, every inch of her sore body protesting the added abuse. She swallowed back a groan, refusing to show any signs of weakness to Reginald or his foul cohorts.

He dismounted and grasped her hair, forcing her to stand. "Meet my intended, gentlemen, the loving creature who carved me up." Reginald held out his blood-encrusted sleeve to the scarred brother. "Grover, I'll require stitches. Tomorrow we'll ride to town to be married by Judge Petrie. Tonight, we need a place to sleep."

The man called Grover smacked his thick lips. "I like me a feisty gal."

Reginald frowned. "She's to remain untouched."

"Too bad," came the reply from the other man. His piggy eyes had remained on Izzy the entire time, making her flesh crawl.

"Keep your hands to yourself, Floyd."

"Bet she's a fighter," Floyd drawled, undeterred by Reginald's warning. His salacious grin revealed tobacco-stained teeth.

Reginald tugged her forward. "While Judge Petrie owes me a huge debt, he's a stickler about not taking a woman by force." He chuckled darkly. "All bets are null once she's my wife."

"Floyd, leave off, now," Grover snapped. He motioned Reginald to follow him toward the ranch porch. "I'll show you where to stash her and then I'll take care of your war wound." He slapped his leg at his own joke.

Still fisting her hair, Reginald marched her over the uneven ground and up the steps. Izzy's eyes watered from his rough treatment, her scalp aching badly.

Leading them down a dim hall, Grover pointed. "In there. Locks from the outside."

Reginald shoved her over the threshold and slammed the door. "Don't try to escape, Isadora. There's nowhere to run. If you somehow managed to get outside, the coyotes would only have you for supper."

Their crude laughter and heavy footsteps faded away.

Weak and sore, Izzy stumbled the short distance to the bed and sank down on one end. Minutes ticked by as she battled overwhelming panic over her predicament, striving to calm herself and slow her pounding heart. Breathing easier at last, she studied the room, opulently furnished, indicating either wealth or thievery. A single window covered in brocaded drapery offered the illusion of freedom. Izzy rose and hurried to pull the expensive fabric aside. A wavy glass pane winked back at her. She ran her bruised fingers along the frame seam, despair flooding her when she found it didn't open.

Releasing the curtain, Izzy backed away.

She'd been imprisoned in a houseful of men with no compunction, no honor. "Lord, what am I to do?" she whispered brokenly.

A voice inside her head answered, "*You are strong and resourceful and will find a way.*" The voice sounded much like Sam's.

New determination and maturity snapped her spine into place. Isadora McDougall might have been a helpless girl, but Izzy Singleton had grit and courage. She'd rise from an untenable situation, and if she could hold to her fortitude those who'd done this to Sam would receive their just comeuppance.

As if in agreement, her energy returned, reminding her she needed food as well as a way to relieve herself. Rooting under the bed netted her a relatively clean chamber pot which she placed in a corner, knowing she'd require it soon. Her stomach rumbled, gnarling hunger the size of a boulder resting there. Her lips felt drier than dust. Would they even bother to bring her food and water?

To take her mind off her own worries, she paced and thought of Sam. "You're alive. I would feel it if you were not," she vowed, stroking the bright amethyst stone on her wedding ring. "Please be alive."

At the sound of the men's voices rising in volume, Izzy tiptoed to the door and pressed her ear to the smooth wood. Remembering Reginald's demand to have his arm stitched, she grinned ferociously at the pain he'd suffer, not nearly enough to satisfy her need for revenge. No doubt he'd drink to dull the feel of the needle.

Maybe he'd pass out from the combination of whiskey and blood loss.

If I remain patient, I could find a way to escape. First, she needed to listen and wait.

A ladderback chair sat along the wall. Izzy strained to lift it, her muscles shaking, and managed to position it against the door. Balancing on the very edge, she kept her ear perked for anything useful, wincing at the muffled, inventive curses, praying Reginald would gulp down enough whiskey to inebriate him fast.

". . . your pretty little filly," one of the men slurred loudly. Were they all drinking? *Even better.*

Izzy held her breath, struggling to hear their conversation. A drunk man was a loose-lipped, boasting man. Reginald, a notorious braggart, might regale them of how he killed her father. Would these men care? *Don't be stupid, they'll no doubt cheer.*

"Clumsy idiot, mind the needle." A pause, then Reginald's foul rejoinder. "Her old man's dead. She's mine now." Even drunk, the self-satisfaction in his tone sickened Izzy.

"Ain't she got a mother?"

Reginald laughed meanly, his next muffled words chilling. "Dead. Husband killed her in a fit of anger, and the son buried her body."

Stark terror and anguish beat down on Izzy until she had to clap both palms over her mouth to hold in her despairing cries. "Mother," she whispered, rocking back and forth, trembling violently.

For what seemed an eternity, she clutched herself in an attempt to remain in control. The proof of her mother's murder repeated in her brain, over and over, mixed with memories of the beautiful woman who'd raised her, loved her.

Pure hatred for her father and brother festered and grew . . . becoming enormous.

Father, already dead, couldn't assuage her thirst for revenge. Her brother, and Reginald Dalton, however, were now fair game. Jumping to her feet, Izzy resumed pacing, searching for a way out. All she needed was a single weakness in her prison walls so she could use it to her advantage.

Her focus returned to the window with its single glass pane, its narrow size not meant for anything other than a way to let in the light. Glass could cut her if she broke it.

I don't give a preacher's damn.

Striding to the bed, Izzy stripped off a pillowcase. If she balled one end of it in her palm, she could wrap the rest around her hand and wrist.

She'd get out of here or die trying.

Chapter 20

"Here, now. Wake up." A hard slap accompanied the raspy command.

Sam groaned and rolled to his side, cracking his lids. Heat radiated down on him from a sweltering sun as nausea twisted inside him. For a moment he feared he'd vomit. A horse must've thrown him, or else sat on his head. He tried to lift an arm to investigate the source of the pain, but the limb felt weighed down.

"What the hell?" he managed, his lips so dry they felt like two twigs rubbing together.

"You been shot. Lucky to be alive. Them buzzards overhead ain't circlin' for sport. I'm gonna sit you up. Don't die on me, y'hear?"

The world spun and tipped as Sam was pulled upright, his belly heaving alarmingly again. He clutched himself and swallowed bile. "Christ."

"I know the feelin'. Puked plenty in my life." A shoulder pushed against Sam's body, keeping him in place while he blinked something wet off his lashes.

A wrinkled bandana was shoved into his hand. "You're still bleedin'."

Weakly, Sam dragged the square of cotton over his forehead where the pain was strongest. Bleary-eyed, he stared at his elderly, grizzled savior. "Hank?"

Hank Soames eyed him closely, frowning. "Nasty looking wound ya got there, Singleton." He held up three fingers. "How many, son?"

"I don't have double vision." Sam coughed to clear his throat. "How long was I out?"

"Couple hours, I reckon." Soames pressed carefully under the torn flesh along Sam's forehead. "Bullet grazed you, clear back to here." He tapped the crown of Sam's head. "If it'd gone in, we wouldn't be havin' this conversation, 'cause you'd be dead." His eyes narrowed. "Got a bead on who shot you?"

"No." An image of Izzy flashed against the overly bright landscape on either side of the trail. He rolled to the edge of the wagon's open edge and swung his legs over the side, wavering on rubbery legs. His gaze landed on a pile of blood-soaked wool a couple feet from the wagon. Additional drops of bright red painted the ground in grisly spatter.

Not Izzy, please, please, not Izzy—

He staggered toward the blanket and grasped one corner, yanking hard, needing to see, yet terrified of what it'd reveal. Discovering a gore-covered head and identifying what was left of William McDougall, his racing heart stabilized. The body already stank to high heaven and had begun to bloat.

"You know who he is?"

"My wife's father."

"Sorry to hear. Found him when I came upon the wagon. Covered him up outta respect for the dead."

Sam dropped the soiled blanket over William's ruined face. "More consideration than the bastard deserved." He held down his gorge with difficulty as he scanned the area for Izzy. "My wife. Where is she?"

"Your wife was here?"

Sam managed a nod, ignoring how the brief movement made his vision wobble. "I have to find her, Soames. She's in grave danger."

"You ain't going anyplace except town. Doc needs to sew you up afore you lose all the blood in your noggin."

"I can't wait around." Sam pushed the older man away. "Rig belongs to Gleason. Help me unhook the team and I'll ride bareback. Can you take the other horse back to town?"

Soames crossed his arms over his skinny chest and planted his feet apart. "Not without you. Listen, I kin see your worry over your lady. Best bet is to round up the sheriff and a posse." He stared Sam down. "*After* you get stitched up. You know I'm right, son."

Sam's fists came up, ready to fight, then he spotted the way they trembled, his legs at the point of collapse beneath him. Damn it, the old coot was right. He'd never make it out on the trail, wouldn't have the sense to track anything, if he didn't get his bleeding under control.

"All right."

Soames nodded sharply. "Smart man. Can you take the leads? I'll toss the body into the wagon bed and follow alongside."

Sam pulled himself onto the seat without help, tamping down his shakes.

His head bursting with pain, he wrapped Soames's bandana around his forehead to keep the blood out of his eyes. "I can make it."

Izzy bided her time.

Judging by the shadows in the room, she'd been locked up for hours. The noise level beyond her prison went from curses to shouts, to slurring half-sentences and then unsettling quiet. Her hope for getting away rested on Reginald and his friends drinking themselves into a stupor.

Waiting for the cover of night meant wandering around in unknown territory while animal predators circled her. A shiver of fright broke her out in gooseflesh. Still, it was better than remaining captive by a cruel man bent on harming her.

The pillowcase she'd taken from the bed worked well as protection, wadded around her knuckles and wrapped past her wrist. Silently she tiptoed to the window and pushed against the glass, testing its strength, finding no weak spots within its narrow opening.

Outside, a full moon rose slowly over the horizon. The light it cast would aid her escape, as well as expose her to Reginald and the Shaw brothers once they figured out she'd run.

I have to try. She'd rather perish in a bid for freedom, than allow Reginald to steal her inheritance and violate her in a sham marriage.

Reluctant to wait any longer, lips smashed together to smother inadvertent exclamations of pain, she swung her fist and punched the window dead center. Glass cracked and broke into chunks with only a soft tinkling instead of the loud crash she'd anticipated.

Shaking off the pieces embedded in the pillowcase, Izzy knocked out what remained, leaving only a few sharp points she couldn't remove protruding from the wood. Hurrying toward the door to retrieve the chair, she brought it to the window and climbed on the seat, stretching her arms through the cleared opening. She groaned when she couldn't squeeze through, her clothing too bulky. Chastising herself for being a ninny, Izzy shed two layers of petticoats and tried again, to no avail.

Weighing the humiliation of running outside half-naked, versus the terrible things Reginald had planned, she unbuttoned her gown and pushed it down her body, leaving her chemise and pantalettes in place. She hadn't bothered with a corset when she'd dressed early in the morning, and now she offered thanks for being in such a hurry to get away from town.

I'd give anything to be there right now, stuffed into my tightest unmentionables if it meant I'd be with Sam.

"Stop it," she chastised, returning to the chair. No good came from feeling sorry for herself. She had to get away and find Sam.

With renewed determination, Izzy started again. Minutes later, after twisting and struggling, she managed to maneuver through the broken window, wincing at the cuts she suffered from leftover glass bits. Dropping to the ground, her leg bent backward and she stifled a cry as her ankle wrenched. Refusing to waste precious seconds catching her breath, she limped from the house, using the moonlight as a guide, unsure of where she was going.

It only mattered she'd escaped.

Sam attached the lantern to his saddle, tightening the straps, and tucking the container of oil in a leather pouch inside his vest. As the others did the same, he glanced over at Frank, clamp-jawed with purpose. The eldest Carter had taken a shine to Izzy, as had most of the folk in town, and volunteered his unique tracking abilities to find her.

I'm damned lucky to have these men on my side.

Joshua edged his stallion close, the animal champing at the bit and stomping a hoof. "You don't look so good, Singleton," he stated bluntly.

"I'm not waiting any longer. Nothing more Doc could do other than stitch me up." Sam forced his creased slouch over the bandages Sheaton had swaddled around his head. It hurt like hell. "I'll be fine."

"Hank said he had to slap you awake a time or two on the road to town," Richard Blackwood put in, guiding his stallion to the other side. His shrewd stare took in Sam from boot to bloodstained hat. "Let me carry your lamp oil, in case you fall off your mount."

"Christ sake, I'm not gonna blow myself up," Sam groused. Richard merely gestured impatiently. Unwilling to waste time arguing, he reached into his vest pocket and handed over the pouch of oil. "Let's ride."

They took the Gulch Mine trail to the north, a rougher ride but also a shorter route to Silver Cache. They'd be in the saddle longer than Sam could bear, his fear for Izzy's safety thrumming through his body with horrendous force, far outpacing the dull pounding in his head.

At the thought of what his young wife might be enduring while they rode, a permanent snarl curled his lip. If Reginald Dalton laid one hand on her, he'd never live to stand trial for his crimes.

By the time they reached the turnoff for Silver Cache, darkness obscured the trail. Estimating it to be close to midnight, Sam kept abreast of Joshua, struggling not to push Lucille, his mare, too hard. They'd already had to slow down on the rocky path to assure none of the horses turned a fetlock or lost a shoe.

Over clattering hooves, Joshua raised his voice to be heard. "Got a telegram from that Marshall in Bolster we asked Lucinda Blackwood about."

Eager for anything that'd take his mind off his never-ending worry, Sam crowded Lucille closer. "And?"

"Fulsome claims Dalton had deep ties to a gang ring called 'Under the Pines.' Thievery, murder, brothels, slavery. Two of their leaders left town before sentencing. Fulsome wasn't all that willing to give out a name, only that he was part of the court convicting them after they tried to bring a Pines brothel to Bolster. Fulsome figured someone on the inside of the law helped them get out of Chicago. Could've been Dalton due to his connections there and knowing where the McDougalls had gone."

"You think Dalton continued an association with these Pines men while following Izzy and her family." It wasn't a question. Sam's innards clenched, barely able to process either Willy or Reginald acquainted with such criminal filth and possibly getting their paws on Izzy.

"I'd say it's a safe bet. I telegraphed Sheriff Blackwood right before you hit town." Joshua patted the pocket of his duster. "He recalls twin brothers coming into Silver Cache now and then for supplies. Apparently his deputy asked them where they lived and got a vague response of them sharing a ranch near Cottonwood Springs, a few miles outside of Silver Cache."

"Why in hell didn't the deputy detain them, ask more questions?" Sam demanded.

"Because they did nothing wrong at the time, Singleton, only came to town and bought some victuals and staples at the feed store in Silver Cache—" Joshua broke off at Frank's shout.

"This way," Frank called, his lantern held aloft. "Deep tracks on the dry. Two riders, one mount, I'd stake my life."

They traveled in tense silence for another good hour, bypassing Silver Cache. Halfway down the trail leading to Cottonwood Springs, Sam spied a ranch house in the distance, silhouetted in the moonlight, hills on one side and deep woods on the other.

Frank doused his lantern. "Best ride in the dark. Rough ground cover here, so mind the rocks." He urged his stallion ahead, its big ebony body indistinguishable against the night.

One by one the others followed, Sam cantering behind Frank, Lucille's soft whinny an accompaniment to the clomping hooves and snorts. Every minute became an eternity as they circled the ranch exterior, its interior completely dark, appearing deserted.

Joshua waved to a cleared area next to a crumbling barn. They dismounted and wasted precious seconds filling their lanterns, Richard returning Sam's oil pouch to him. Matchsticks at the ready and guns drawn, with no way of knowing what they were up against, they bent low, using scrub and spots of high grass to mask their approach.

Sam in the lead, they came around the back side of the ranch, and his gut clenched at the sight of a gaping window. He lit his lantern, holding it up, detecting glass sparkling in the soft light. Stepping closer, he peered inside the room.

A crumpled-up dress and petticoats littered the floor among bigger chunks of glass.

"Izzy was in there," Sam mouthed to them, beckoning Richard to follow him. Waving to Joshua and Frank, he pointed toward the barn and surrounding buildings.

Joshua nodded sharply, then he and Frank sprinted toward the barn.

Sam strode for the front entrance of the ranch with Blackwood right behind him, and they stealthily climbed the steps. He put his ear to the front door, registering only silence from within.

Carefully disengaging the latch, Sam swung the door open and eased inside. A quick scan indicated the main room was empty. A large square table sat in the middle. It held two bottles of liquor, both nearly empty, and three tumblers.

Crossing the room, he focused on a reddish-streaked pail of water on the floor near the table, with a stained spool of waxed thread tossed next to it. A bloody rag hung out of the pail, a gore-studded needle sticking from the tattered cotton.

Dread squeezed his heart.

Coming alongside him, Richard seemed to read his mind. "Doesn't mean it's hers, Sam."

Sam nodded grimly, the movement causing him to wince against the stitches Doc Sheaton had used on his gunshot wound. Turning to search the rest of the ranch, he found only emptiness. The last room held locks that bolted from the outside, the door wide open. Besides an overturned chair and Izzy's discarded clothing, he found some shredded, dark-tinged linen caught on a jagged nub of glass from the window she'd obviously escaped from.

"Your woman got away." Approval coated the sheriff's tone.

Pride swelled in Sam's chest at Izzy's bravery. Whatever she'd gone through, he would help her heal. The most important thing was finding her alive. The fact she'd been locked away from the men, and had escaped, gave him hope she hadn't been harmed.

They left to join Joshua and Frank out front.

Frank gripped Sam's shoulder. "Looks like two riders headed out not too long ago, following Izzy's footprints. Another went in the direction of Silver Cache."

"Odd," Richard mused.

"Doesn't change anything." Ignoring the agony behind his eyes, Sam sprinted for his horse. "We need to find Izzy, damn it."

He just hoped they weren't already too late.

Chapter 21

The woods, edging the pasture where the Shaws' ranch house stood, had seemed like the best place to hide, and Izzy had trekked in that direction as fast as her injury would allow. Her chemise had torn in several places and her stockings were shredded as the thin silk caught on twisted bushes and brittle grasses.

During the first few hours of her escape, the full moon had lit her way. The sounds of animals had kept her moving at a steady pace, afraid a pack of coyotes would attack her in search of food as Reginald had threatened.

Her limp had grown worse, her ankle swollen against the laces holding the beautiful slippers Sam had bought her. She dared not loosen anything for fear she'd never get them back onto her feet. Their thin soles were insufficient against the rough ground cover, the satiny uppers torn and tattered, with holes leaving spots of her feet bare. Each step became more and more difficult as blisters formed and popped. The thistle she'd gotten snarled in hurt horribly, minuscule thorns still embedded in her ankles.

She stumbled as weakness assailed her limbs. It'd been hours since she'd escaped and the men would have surely discovered her absence by now as sunrise streaked the sky red-orange and illuminated every shadow. Stumbling across a small stream a while back, she'd drunk as much as she dared and splashed herself, worried her cramping belly would purge anything she tried to swallow.

The sun rose fast, as if to mock her, its overhead heat sucking moisture from her body, even as sweat dripped down her face. She impatiently shoved back a damp curl.

Her energy dwindling, Izzy desperately searched the area for a safe place to hide where she could regain her strength before continuing. Foothills of prairie stretched ahead, mostly grassland, with jutting fallen rocks scattered amongst low brush and young trees. Fear pounding through her veins, she forced her tired legs to keep moving in that direction. With each step, her chest heaved with ragged breaths.

What would Reginald do if he caught her? He couldn't kill her, or he'd never get control of her inheritance. That didn't mean he wouldn't hurt her.

Attaining the lower woods seemed to take forever. Her muscles throbbed with exhaustion by the time she found enough shade and protection in the form of roughly clumped trees with thin leaves, growing close to the ground. It would have to do; she couldn't travel another foot. Crawling beneath the larger of the trees, Izzy ignored the way the dry grasses scratched her skin. Curling into a ball, she used her hands as a pillow and closed her eyes.

Sam's image immediately flashed across her mind, ripping an anguished cry from deep within her. *Is he still alive?* She couldn't bear it if he'd perished.

Unable to hold back tears any longer, hard sobs claimed her.

Izzy didn't know how much time passed before she'd cried herself out. By the way the sun's heat poured down on her with blinding force, she'd probably dozed as well. What paltry shade she'd found earlier now gone, sweat drenched her entire body. She wrinkled her nose against her own stink.

God, what I wouldn't give for a cool bath and a tall glass of water.

An image of Dolores's chess pie popped in her mind and her stomach gurgled with sharp, shooting pangs of hunger. How long had it been since she'd eaten? After learning of what she imagined was her husband's duplicity, she'd lost her appetite and had gone to bed with no supper. The next morning she'd barely picked at her breakfast.

Foolish girl! Remembering how she'd doubted Sam, shame almost knocked her flat. *Get up,* she scolded. If she didn't keep moving, she'd soon be nothing but buzzard bait. With a groan, Izzy forced herself upright.

Squinting, she shaded her eyes against the sunlight with one hand and tried to figure out which way to go. Confusion scrambled her brain until she could no more get her bearings than fly in the right direction. Choosing a path running along the foothills, Izzy hoped it would lead her to a town instead of back to the ranch from where she'd fled.

What seemed like an eternity passed, but the sun's location indicated it'd only been an hour at best. Her energy flagged with each step she took, every muscle in her body rejecting the idea of traveling any further.

Knowing Sam would not want her to give up, she pushed aside her exhaustion and pain and trudged on.

With only a narrow path to follow, she'd been at the mercy of rabbit holes and gopher hills, tripping over several as she entered the place where pasture and woods converged. Izzy gritted her teeth against each new pain and kept going. Her feet had long ago grown numb. Every time a coyote had howled or an owl hooted, she froze in fear.

Using tree trunks for cover, Izzy ventured deeper, scared she'd lose her way as the thick leaf canopies overhead cast a shadow over the foliage and made everything appear the same. She doggedly kept going, confident she'd eventually stumble upon a cabin or perhaps a mine, where people could help her. Any other outcome was unacceptable.

Sudden shouts echoed over the pasture edging the tree line. Biting back a cry, Izzy hid, using a wide-trunked juniper to shield herself. Straining to decipher the direction of her enemies, she focused on each crunch of feet on leaves. They seemed to come from everywhere.

She pressed her mouth against her knees to hold in her urge to scream. For an indeterminable time she waited, hardly drawing breath, then raised her head at the heavy silence. Had they passed by? Was she safe?

She peered around the tree trunk, the dimness making it difficult to see anything beyond where she huddled. Nothing except the swoosh of her pounding blood reached her ears.

Cautiously, she straightened, hating the thought of putting weight on her feet, knowing she couldn't remain here any longer—

A rough hand grabbed her arm and yanked her up. Izzy's shriek ended on a sob when her damaged ankle turned under her, sending sharp pains up her leg.

Frantically, she tried to break free. The grip tightened and tugged her against a hard body that stank of whiskey.

"Caught you." Reginald held on to her despite her frenzied struggles. He shook her until her teeth rattled.

Tears of defeat spilled over her lashes.

The dappled shade did nothing to hide the cold anger in her captor's eyes. The Shaw brother with the scar laughed as Reginald panted, "You're going to pay for this infraction, Isadora."

With a desperate cry, Izzy broke free and whirled from them, hobbling clumsily, ignoring the agony in her feet and body. Reginald's threats filled the air along with the sound of horses' hooves quickly closing the distance.

In her heart, she knew there would be no escape for her, but she had to try. The faster they gained on her, the stronger her fury grew. Right before they reached her, Izzy snatched a large rock off the ground and turned to confront them, struggling for breath. "Stay back!"

Their amusement only increased her anger.

"She's gonna be a fun one to tame. Sure you don't want some help with that?"

Reginald's scowling demeanor didn't bode well. "If she rebels again, Grover, I'll consider it." He wiped sweat off his upper lip as he glared at her. "You're a lot of trouble, Isadora."

"Then let me go."

"Not after all I've gone through to get you."

Izzy's legs trembled so badly she could scarcely stand. "You're a rich man. Why do you care about a little money I inherited?" She fisted the rock until it cut into her palm. "Don't you have enough of your own?"

"Oh, it's more than a little money, dear girl." A ghoulish grin lit his face, making him look like the devil himself. "A fortune, Isadora. Your grandfather left your mother a fortune in a trust fund only she could access. He made it plain in his will that if anything happened to his daughter, it all went to you." He chuckled. "Evidently, the old codger was smart enough to know your father and Willy would only squander it."

Her brows scrunched. "Why would Father give you anything?"

His repulsive stare never leaving her, he swung a leg over his horse's back and dismounted. "Years ago, William lost a great deal of money at one of my gambling establishments in Chicago. I was kind enough to allow him to pay it off, with interest, over the years. But after he killed your mother, his card-playing talents worsened." He shrugged. "I've had my eye on you for a long time, sweetheart. When your father offered both you and your family's inheritance in exchange for forgiving his remaining debt along with a yearly stipend, I couldn't refuse."

He pointed to the ground in front of him. "Now, get over here."

"Go to hell." She grasped the rock tighter in preparation of throwing it at his loathsome face.

Suddenly, a rope looped over her shoulders and tightened, trapping her arms to her sides. The rock dropped uselessly to the ground.

Her gaze flew to Grover Shaw. He'd lassoed her like a calf. Eyeing her lecherously, he tossed the other end to Reginald, who caught it deftly, and with a rough yank made her stumble forward.

"I sent Floyd to town to bring the Judge back out to the ranch, Isadora," he gloated. "We're getting married today."

"No," she cried, digging in her heels.

Grover continued to laugh as Reginald tugged at the rope, reeling her in. As hard as she tried to resist, Izzy didn't have the strength. All too soon she stood directly in front of him.

Filled with hate and unable to defend herself, Izzy gathered what little moisture she could from her parched mouth and spat on him.

"I don't know, Reggie." Grover rubbed his scraggly, filthy chin. "She might be more'un you can handle. Sure you don't want me and Floyd to tame her for you?"

With a foul oath, Reginald's fist shot toward her. Trapped by the rope, she couldn't dodge the blow, her head rocking back sharply at the vicious punch which caught her high on the cheek.

Instantly she went blind in her right eye as a pained groan burst from her lips.

"That's just a prelude of your upcoming punishment, Isadora." He pushed her over to his horse and roughly tossed her onto the stallion before climbing up behind her.

Removing his slouch, Sam swiped at his sweaty forehead with the back of his sleeve. Frank had lost Izzy's trail a few miles back in a lush field of prairie grass, but still felt confident they were moving in the right direction. "We're gonna need to stop and water the horses. Let them rest a bit."

He slapped his hat back on, hating the thought of slowing down the search for any reason. If they didn't take care of the animals soon, they'd be walking, which would reduce their chance of finding Izzy before Dalton did.

"There's a watering hole not far ahead," Richard said.

"That's right," Frank agreed. "We ran across it a few years back when we were searching for Addie."

Sam's eyebrows reached for the sky. "Addie? Retta's girl went missing?"

"This was before Knight moved to the area." Joshua's voice held a hard edge. "A criminal by the name of Slim Morgan took her."

"I've heard the name a time or two." Sam glanced over at Joshua. "Wasn't he your boy's father?"

"Was," Joshua retorted briefly. "I'm Nate's pa now."

"Morgan committed plenty of crimes around here, kidnapping the least of it," Frank put in. "Killed a few good men, too, on top of what he did to the young'uns."

Joshua edged closer. "It's a long story. Let's just say the bastard was hard to kill, but not impossible." His tone held satisfaction.

For the next few minutes, Frank recounted Slim Morgan's sins and his dramatic ending, until they reached the sparkling stream. While the others dismounted to refill their canteens, Sam knelt next to his fractious mare and stroked her flank reassuringly, murmuring to her, relieved when she settled. Cupping a handful of the cool liquid, he rinsed off the back of his neck before scooping up more to quench his thirst. He shoved his canteen into the stream until it was full, then stood to tuck it back into his saddlebag.

"Sam," Frank called out from downstream, "I found her tracks."

He spun and dashed to where Frank knelt. Though he wasn't a tracker himself, Sam recognized Izzy's footprints.

"Looks like her feet are bleeding." Frank touched one of the dark spots.

Dried speckles stood out like rust near the dirt impression of her heels and toes. Tension tightened his already rock-hard shoulders, the ache in his head intensifying. "How long ago?"

Joshua and Blackwood joined them.

"Couple hours, I reckon." Frank rose to his feet. Sam followed him downstream, along with both lawmen. Pausing, Frank pointed at more tracks. "Looks like two riders are about an hour behind her."

"C'mon then," Sam snapped, hope buoying him as he rushed to his horse. "Let's get moving."

They rode away from the stream, Izzy's tracks leading them along Bountiful's foothills and its spots of fallen rock and woods.

Frank pointed off to his left. "This way. Looks like Dalton is gaining ground on her."

Sam's mouth tightened, and he flicked his reins to get Lucille moving fast. "We need to pick up the pace."

No one argued and they covered a goodly distance, until Richard held up a hand. "Hold up, gentlemen."

"What is it?" Frank asked.

He turned to Frank with a finger to his lips, at the same time a man's laugh floated across the breeze, followed by the sound of Dalton's ugly gloat of, "This time tomorrow you'll be my wife."

"You're crazy," came the sharp retort, "if you think that. Sam's going to kill you for what you've done."

"And you're delusional. Singleton is dead."

Joshua gestured for them to take cover, each man climbing from their horse to find shelter.

Sam led his mare to a tall bristlecone, ground-hitching her near the trunk. Crouching next to a clump of sage, he waited.

Two men on horseback rounded a short bend, one of them Reginald Dalton, Izzy slumped in the saddle in front of him. She'd been abused, her body battered and marked with bruises, one of her eyes swollen completely shut.

Tattered underclothes, streaked with dirt and splotches of blood, were all that protected her nudity. Dalton clutched her around the waist tightly enough to cut off her air supply, one fist a mere inch or so from her breast.

The fury Sam had managed to hold at bay ignited like a prairie fire and scorched through his body. His nostrils flared.

You're a dead man, Dalton.

Fighting to hold back the howl of outrage burning him raw, Sam drew his Colt from its holster. Joshua, poised next to Richard behind a large boulder, shot Sam a warning glare to stand down.

Frank hunkered off to the side, sheltered from view of the riders by brush and foliage. He held up five fingers and started counting down as the men approached.

Five. Four. Three.

Richard's stallion whinnied, giving away their presence.

Everything happened at once.

The unknown man dropped off the side of his mount, coming to his feet, pistol in hand. Blackwood rolled from behind a tree and raised his weapon at the same time Joshua rushed out with his rifle and shouted, "You're surrounded. Throw down your guns."

Dalton, using Izzy as a shield, held a deadly-looking revolver to her temple. "Stay back!"

The unknown man began shooting, Joshua and Richard returning fire.

Sam didn't wait to see the outcome. Instead he ran, dodging trees, and worked his way around the unfolding scene, stealing up to the hindquarters of Dalton's stallion so quietly, the beast never shifted a hoof.

Movement to the right caught his eye, and Sam raised his Colt. Frank had edged around his coverage, his shotgun leveled on Dalton. The unknown man lay face-down, bleeding, while Joshua tended to Richard, wounded but thankfully conscious. Sam snapped his focus back to protecting his wife.

"Stop right there, Dalton," Frank ordered. "I swear to God I'll shoot your horse if I have to. You're not leaving with Izzy."

"Do you know who I am?" Dalton snapped. "I can have you and your entire family killed in your sleep and you'd never see my men coming. Now get the hell out of my way."

Frank cocked both barrels of his powerful Avery. "Don't think so." He aimed dead center of Dalton's chest. "I'm fixin' to widen your ribs, asshole."

While Frank had the man's attention, Sam sidled closer, reaching for Izzy's arm. With a quick tug, he pulled her from the horse. Tucking his body around her, he rolled them beneath a fallen tree, lifting his head to prepare for any approaching danger.

Weapons now trained on him, Dalton had no place to go. Cursing, he kicked his mount in the flank and started firing wildly, bullets going harmlessly wide. The startled horse bolted, Frank barely jumping out of the way before getting trampled.

Losing his balance, Dalton tumbled off the tall stallion, one fancy boot spur tangling in the stirrup. The panicked animal dragged him across brush and rocks.

Impassively Sam watched, holding Izzy against his shoulder to shield her from witnessing the man's inevitable demise, his frantic cries for help abruptly silenced when his head struck a large boulder with a thud and splattered like an overripe pumpkin.

Chapter 22

Bone-weary, Izzy floated in and out of sleep during the ride back to Little Creede, voices coming to her amidst muffled hooves and the smooth rhythm of a horse beneath her. After many hours of terror, the comfort of her husband's safe embrace allowed her to doze peacefully.

After being torn from Reginald's horse, she'd realized the body protecting her on the hard ground belonged to Sam. While bullets whizzed in the air, the steady beat of his heart had been the answer to her prayers.

Izzy pried open an eyelid and bit back a whimper. The other eye pounded like a toothache, courtesy of the punch she'd taken from Reginald Dalton.

I'm glad he's dead.

She shifted on the saddle, moaning as her sore muscles protested. Swaddled in Sam's duster, he held her firmly against his chest. "Shh . . ." He dropped a kiss to the top of her head. "I've got you. Go back to sleep. We're almost home."

Nodding—at least she thought she did—Izzy allowed herself to relax. "I love you," she mumbled, needing him to know, so thankful she could say the words now. Yawning, she snuggled closer.

His tender, "I love you too, Izzy," was the last thing she heard as sleep took her under.

The next time she awoke, Sam was carrying her down the hallway leading to the private suites in the Galleria. Too tired to keep her eyes open, familiar voices floated around her.

"Poor child," Hannah murmured, followed by Knight's rumbling anger.

"Ah'd like to git mah hands on that scallywag brother of hers." His voice dropped lower. "Territorial's a fittin' place fer the bastard."

Whatever Hannah said in response, Izzy's fuddled brain couldn't decipher. She wanted to reassure her dear friends she was unharmed for the most part but hadn't the energy to speak.

Her head resting on Sam's broad shoulder, Izzy drifted, trying not to cling when he placed her on their bed even as she relished the pure relief of something soft against her battered limbs. Vaguely she heard him ask, "How about a nice bath?"

"Yes, please."

Minutes or hours later, she found herself being gently stripped of her filthy, torn undergarments, biting her lip when his ministrations hit a bad bruise. "Sorry." Sam pressed a gentle kiss against the damaged skin. "I'm going to lift you and set you in the tub." He slipped his arms beneath her legs. "Don't go back to sleep now."

Warm water, wonderfully refreshing, swirled over her and she almost purred with relief. "Oh, that feels good."

Moments later, rustling clothing and sloshing water roused her from her light doze. Sam eased himself under her body, urging her to rest against him. "Let's just soak for a while, all right?" he said gently. "Dolores is making poultices for your feet and your eye."

At the feel of her husband's strong, naked body beneath her, something inside her fully relaxed, and she released a sigh of contentment. Needing to reassure herself he was truly with her and not some figment of wishful delirium, Izzy resettled so she could look up at him.

"You're really here." She ran her fingers along his bristled jaw, loving the roughness. Blinking to clear her vision, she touched the dirty bandage around his head. "Let me see."

"Honey, I'm fine. Doc stitched me up. Said I'll probably have a scar, so I suppose I'll let my hair grow long and flop it over whatever bald spot I end up with." Humor laced his tone. "I'll give Sheriff Lang a run for his money."

Izzy couldn't share in his amusement, having witnessed the way his broad, muscled frame had slammed into the wagon seat when Reginald's bullet hit him. She'd surely see it in her sleep for months, years, to come. "It's not funny, Mister Singleton. You could have died."

"And so could you, Missus Singleton. Do you think I was any less frightened when I came to and realized you were gone? When I saw for myself the condition—" He bit off his own protest. Against her temple she could feel his hard swallow. "I need to know. Did any of those bastards—?"

"No, oh, no." She tried to turn but he crossed his arms over her breasts, holding her firmly in place. "I swear, they didn't."

His oath of, "Thank God," held such relief.

When she continued to squirm, he rumbled, "Settle down, now. We're both alive and safe. Nothing else matters. Agreed?"

At his sensible rejoinder, most of the tension left her body. She caught the edge of his chin in a kiss. "Agreed."

They soaked for a while longer. Sam produced a cake of soap and a soft cloth which he used to gently wash the grime from her skin. Each time he touched a particularly bruised spot, he'd apologize, brushing soft kisses along the side of her neck.

Despite his protests for her to remain still, Izzy got hold of the cloth and soaped him in return, her usual shyness at his nakedness buried beneath her desire to care for him as he'd done for her.

Face to face at last in the cooling water, his hard length against her hip was at once a comfort and a temptation, as she patted the cloth over his swollen forehead. "Tell me if I hurt you."

Curving one large palm around her neck, he brought her in for a tender kiss. "You could never hurt me. Unless you stopped loving me the way I love you."

"Never." Abandoning the soap, Izzy flung her arms around his neck, uncaring she splashed water over the side of the tub. "I'll always love you, Sam."

He stared deeply into her eyes. "You hold my heart, Izzy. Today and forever."

In the sitting parlor of the Galleria, Sam enjoyed the sight of his lovely wife holding Knight and Hannah's tiny son, crooning softly to him as he alternately fussed and then draped over her shoulder with the sort of world-weary sigh only an infant could produce.

Uncomfortable at the thought of letting her out of his sight, Sam stood next to her, one hand toying with her curls, After their shared bath the night before, he'd applied Dolores' salve mixture to Izzy's damaged feet, wrapping them in linen then covering the medicine with a pair of his boot hose to keep the stuff from staining anything. He'd wanted her to rest but his wife had other ideas. When he'd placed her on the bed, she'd drawn him down for a kiss. Caressed him. Whispered how much she needed him.

Unable to deny her pleas or his own urgent demands to have his wife beneath him again, alive and well, Sam carefully joined their bodies, intending to exert strict temperance and show her only gentleness. Until she wound herself around him like satin ropes. "I'm not made of glass, Sam."

When she'd licked his throat and nipped him, he'd pretty much lost his mind and most of his control. His ardent wife had arched eagerly beneath him as he loved her, until their shared passion flung them over the precipice together.

Now, dressed in a loose-fitting gown in deference to her bruises, Izzy's injuries stood out in stark relief against her normally creamy complexion. Her eye, not as swollen thanks to the salve, nevertheless sported a ring of dark purplish-blue.

Every time his gaze locked on her injuries, his red-hot anger coiled tighter and tighter. If he could have brought Dalton back to life so he could kill the sick bastard with his bare hands, Sam would have gladly suffered the consequences.

Hannah poured tea while Knight fidgeted with an unlit cigar. One side glance from her had him sheepishly stowing it in his vest pocket.

"Ah promised mah bride ah'd leave off the cigars fer a bit, but ah'll tell yew, Sam, if evah a man needed a smoke, it'd be from these past days." Knight took out a pristine handkerchief and blotted the back of his neck. "Yew care to join me?"

Sam stroked Izzy's silky hair, letting the tendrils sift through his fingers, unable to bear stepping outside for a cigar with his employer and friend, though his rational mind told him his wife was safe. His inner panic had yet to ease, and it'd be a while before he could leave her alone.

His expression must have been telling, because Knight emitted a snort of amusement. "Ah kin see that'd be a big ol' naw." He slapped Sam's shoulder hard enough to knock him over. Sam held his feet amidst giggles from Izzy and Hannah. "Ah do understand. The need to protect our womenfolk an' young'uns, why, it's a powerful thing."

"Yes, it is." Sam nodded toward a liquor credenza set up along the rear wall. "Perhaps not a cigar right now, but I'll gladly have a drink."

"Ah do believe ah'll join yew." Knight led the way.

After several glances to assure Izzy was comfortable with Hannah and the babe, Sam followed. Retrieving a pair of squat crystal tumblers, he measured out two fingers of bourbon for each. He raised his glass and tapped it to Knight's. "Cheers. May our lives finally settle."

"Ah'll drink to that, suh." Knight downed his and smacked his lips. Reaching for the decanter, he splashed more into his tumbler. "Ah heard one of them Shaw scallywags run off an' the other got hisself shot in the ass."

"Yeah." Sam set his drink on the credenza. "Got kinda confusing as to whether Richard or Joshua shot the man. But I do believe the bullet entered his sittin' down area."

Knight emitted a bark of glee. "Serve the bugger right fer takin' up with trash like Dalton." Then he sobered, glancing over at where Izzy and Hannah sat together. "Kin he be held fer anythin'?"

"No, unless basic stupidity is a crime, plus we can't prove intent. Joshua had to let him go. I figure the man went off to meet up with his brother. Maybe they'll return to that ranch in Cottonwood Springs. If they're smart they'll go find somewhere else to live and stay out of trouble. And they'd better hope Richard gets back on his feet, soon. At least the bullet didn't hit his shootin' arm." Sam downed the rest of his drink, waving off Knight's offer for another. "One's my limit today."

Thinking about the Shaws, he mused, "You know, I suspect they might actually be the men Joshua told me about. Escaped prosecution in Chicago and nobody can say where they went, including the sheriff back in Ohio who sent Joshua the telegram. With no proof, there's not much we can do but keep an eye on them."

"Then we'll git 'er done, yessir. An' if'n they evah slip up, ah got plenty of persuasion, ain't ah?" Knight patted his holster. "Fer now, ah'm right glad yer lil' gal is safe—"

A commotion at the front of the lobby cut him off.

Sam instinctively reached for his holster before remembering he'd left it off this morning because he thought they'd be safe.

I'm an idiot. He spun toward the entryway, spotting Izzy's good-for-nothing brother.

Disheveled and obviously inebriated, Willy McDougall slurred, "Izzsadora, come wit' me, now."

The man waved a pistol in the air, then used it to gesture to his sister who'd risen from the sofa. "I'm not going anywhere with you, Willy." She crossed her arms and glared at him.

Sam strode toward her, freezing in place when Willy shakily swung the pistol toward her. Damnation, he couldn't take a chance on her safety when a drunk, armed fool pointed a gun only a few yards away. Hannah clambered to her feet with the babe, backing toward Knight who wrapped a burly arm around her waist and whisked her from the lobby.

Relieved they were out of harms' way, Sam drew Willy's attention off Izzy. "McDougall, lay it down before you do something you'll regret."

"I sure as hell ain't gonna regret killin' me a traitor or two," Willy shouted, bug-eyed and crazed-looking. The pistol he held wavered but Sam didn't dare attempt rushing in for his wife. Thankfully she remained still, her defiance obvious as she stared unblinkingly at her unstable brother.

"Willy," she began evenly, "you don't want to rot in prison. Father's gone, Dalton is dead. You can go back to Chicago and start over—"

"With what? My stellar looks?" Willy snarled. "I've got *nothing*. You think the Pines organization wants me back? I'll be lucky if they don't slap a nice, big target on my back and a price on my head." He lurched sideways and every muscle in Sam's body bunched, ready to disarm him when the chance arose. Somehow, Willy was able to steady his pistol, leveling it straight at Izzy's head.

"Honey, don't move," Sam whispered, trusting her to obey as he maintained unfaltering focus on her brother.

Spotting John Washburn, repeater in hand, silently advancing from the door behind Willy, Sam could only offer a blink of acknowledgement.

Willy cocked his pistol, leaving Sam no choice but to act. He leapt for Izzy, taking her to the floor, curving his body around hers. His limbs took most of the jolt as he rolled her beneath him to shield her.

The report of Willy's pistol rang in his ears, followed by a loud thump and a shower of plaster. Izzy clung to him, quivering violently.

Knight shouted, "Ah got rope."

Izzy pushed at his chest, attempting to see around him. "Who's been shot?"

John called out, "He's down, Sam. It's over."

Satisfied that McDougall was rendered harmless, Sam got to his feet and helped Izzy up.

While Knight took care of Willy, John approached. "Sorry 'bout that. When I knocked the gun out of the bastard's hand it went off, and the bullet ripped out a chunk of ceiling."

Relieved Izzy wasn't hurt, Sam pulled her in for a hug. His tension abated when her arms came around his waist and she hugged him back. "I'm damned weary of being shot at," he admitted with a grunt.

Her heartfelt, "Me, too," brought a faint smile to his lips.

She edged around Sam. "I need to talk to my brother."

"Wait first," he cautioned, checking to assure Knight had trussed Willy's hands and feet up nice and snug. With John armed and standing at the ready, the discharged pistol kicked across the floor, Sam stepped aside, knowing she deserved to confront her only remaining relative.

Izzy came forward with no trace of the shy, scared girl Sam remembered from only weeks ago. It took effort for him to allow her within a foot of Willy, now propped against a table, his countenance twisted and hateful. Knight's threatening presence and John's cocked repeater kept Sam from snatching her up to carry her away from any fresh danger.

"I don't know what I did to make you despise me," Izzy began calmly. "I always looked up to you, Willy. Finding out you helped Father with . . ." She faltered and swallowed hard. "I'll not speak of it. You know what you did, and you'll go to prison for it. You'll have a good, long time to reflect on your crimes."

"You've always been worthless," Willy retorted, "you and Mother both. If she hadn't lorded over Father how she controlled the purse strings, she might still be alive." His lips pinched shut on the rest of his vitriol when the muzzle of John's Winchester pushed against his ear.

Izzy's eyes grew bright with unshed emotion as she turned her back on her brother. "I have nothing more to say."

Sam opened his arms and she stepped into them, tucking close. "Are you all right?" He tightened his embrace.

She nodded once.

"I'm proud of you, Izzy Singleton."

EPILOGUE

Two months later

Kneeling in the newly-turned earth, Izzy reinforced the base of the rose shrub, avoiding its thorns. "It's straight now. You can let go."

Beside her, Sam released the stake tied to the young plant. "Hannah says it'll bloom from May to the first frost." He brushed dirt from his sleeves. "She donated some burlap and linen to wrap around it for the winter."

"Everyone's been so kind." Izzy traced the name Jack Jaworski had etched onto the silver plate mounted on the cross. "Mother loved roses. She'd have loved this marker, too."

She sat back on her heels, unwilling to leave quite yet, and glanced at Sam, waiting patiently. "Just a few more minutes?"

"Whatever you want, honey. Take all the time you need." He leaned in for a kiss, gentle and sweet on her lips, then got to his feet, clasping his hat to his chest in deference to the departed souls who populated the cemetery of Reverend Matias's church.

Ten days had passed since Sam and Joshua had taken Knight's buckboard to Silver Cache to collect her mother's remains, found in the root cellar of the house where Izzy had lived. A month after Territorial Prison guards took Willy away, he'd finally confessed to his part in their mother's murder.

Once Joshua received the telegram from Territorial, he and Sam had wasted no time loading up the buckboard with shovels.

Izzy'd wanted to go. Sam wouldn't let her.

"We'll be careful and respectful, Izzy," he'd promised, holding her back when she tried to climb into the wagon.

"She's my mother, Sam."

"You don't want to see her like this. Wouldn't you rather remember her the way she used to be?"

He was right, she'd conceded. When the buckboard returned a few days later, it carried a whitewashed pine coffin. Tears were shed but the better memories remained in Izzy's mind.

With a final caress to the wooden cross Hank Soames had taken such care to carve, Izzy stood, shaking out her skirts, Sam instantly at her side.

She clutched his elbow and managed a smile. "I'm ready to go home, but I'd like to visit, now and then."

"We'll both visit, if that's all right by you." He guided her to the path leading to town.

"I'd like that, Sam."

"This harvest dance was a marvelous idea." Catherine beamed at Sam and Hannah. "Now, let me see that sweet bundle of joy." She held out her arms for Alexander, who had woken from his nap and fussed crossly.

Stifling a yawn, Hannah passed her the babe. "Be my guest. He's started teething, too soon in my opinion. Kept me up most of the night." She handed Catherine a scrap of knotted muslin soaked in water. "Rub this against his gums if the need arises."

Catherine jiggled the tiny boy carefully on one shoulder, grinning when he calmed and rested against her limply. "It's all in the wrist, Missus Gleason."

"Of course, he'd not fall asleep for his mama. Contrary rascal." Hannah regarded her son with love. "Careful, Catherine, he'll drool all over your lovely gown."

"I don't mind." Catherine kissed the babe's downy red tuft.

Hannah turned her attention to Sam, who tried to stem his amusement. "Your turn will come one of these days, mark my words."

"If you say so." He cleared his throat. "I wanted to thank you both for doing this." He nodded toward Izzy, currently being danced across the floor by an exuberant Knight, while Dub Blackwood and Tucker Phelps played a rousing Irish reel. "It's taken my wife's mind off her family woes, and for that I'm eternally grateful."

"This town looks for any excuse to have a party, I guarantee." Catherine gingerly laid Alexander back into his mother's arms. Instantly he awoke and burst into noisy sobs. "Uh-oh." She produced a sympathetic mien, yet anyone who knew her saw the devilment beyond the pursed lips and cheerful, "I can take him back, Hannah."

"No, she can't," Frank announced, popping up next to his wife. "Dance with me, darlin'." He swept her away as Tucker began strumming a slower version of "Wildwood Flower."

Sam held out both hands. "Give him here, Miss Hannah, and go spend some time with your husband."

"You don't have to offer twice," she replied laughingly, placing her son into Sam's care. Immediately Alexander quieted, shoved an entire fist in his mouth, and fell asleep. Hannah sighed. "See? Contrary. Just like his papa."

"Yes, ma'am." He snuggled the precious infant, rocking back and forth, while Hannah approached Knight and Izzy smilingly relinquished the big, brash gambler to his diminutive wife.

Izzy crossed the makeshift dance floor, smoothing her wayward curls, longer now and brushing the tops of her shoulders. Her hair ribbon was askew, her skin dewy from trying to keep up with Knight's fancy footwork. In that moment Sam thought he'd never seen a more beautiful sight.

He wanted her to have everything in the world; replace all she had lost over the years.

Starting now.

She met his stare with an arched brow. "You look quite serious." She eyed the babe thoughtfully. "Did Alexander fill up his diaper? I can change him—"

"I need to show you something." His voice came out gruffer than intended. Both her brows shot up as he amended, "Nothing bad."

"All right," she replied slowly.

Once the song had ended, Sam returned Alexander to his folks and led Izzy out of the main salon, toward the roulette room. A few lamps had been left lit, illuminating the ornate wheel and felt-covered table, the heavy drapes at each window, and the chaises scattered here and there throughout. Sam brought her over to one corner where the Galleria's prized Steinway had been relocated to make room for a dance area in the salon.

Izzy touched several white keys. "It's truly a magnificent instrument."

"It's yours, Missus Singleton."

"M-Mine?" She whirled to him so wildly, he had to steady her upper arms to keep her from toppling. She hung in his grasp, open-mouthed.

"Yours," he said, enjoying her reaction.

"I don't understand. How can this be mine?" She trembled beneath his palms.

"Let's sit down, and I'll tell you everything." He led her to one of the chaises, drawing her into his arms once they were seated. "This past spring, Knight and I discussed opening another gambling casino, going in as partners. Rocky Gulch is growing fast, so last week he bought acreage outside of town that the Carter brothers owned and were willing to sell. We'll break ground in March, maybe April, and start building."

"What does that have to do with the Steinway piano?"

"I bought acreage in Rocky Gulch, too. The piano will be the first piece of furniture going into our new house."

"You *bought* me a Steinway?" Her eyes had grown huge and dark. "But we haven't received our first deposit from my grandfather's trust yet. How can we afford it?"

Recalling the Gleasons' stubbornness, Sam smiled. "I was going to buy it for you, but after I told Knight how your mother gave you lessons, and your love of playing, he and Hannah insisted you have it. I had difficulty accepting it for free, so we settled on one silver dollar."

She blinked up at him. Her mouth opened and closed, before her eyes widened and she said hoarsely, "H-House?"

His sweetheart must have finally recalled what he'd said after 'piano.' Sam's grin widened. "House."

"And a Steinway."

He kissed the corner of her mouth. "Yes. Knight and Hannah adore you, Izzy. Let them do this for you."

For long moments she seemed to struggle with such a generous gesture, then she melted into his arms, tilting her head to stare at the polished instrument several yards away. "I have to do something to repay such generosity." She looked up with earnest, blurry eyes. "You'll help me think of something, won't you? Perhaps a place where impoverished children can learn to play music. Or just learn to be happy again. A sort of halfway point between being orphaned and fostered. Even better, adopted someday. It's not like we couldn't afford it."

"A true statement if I ever heard one," Sam replied, awed by his wife's generous, thoughtful nature. "We'll work on it together."

"Together," Izzy echoed, her attention returning to the glossy piano. "It's so beautiful."

"Yes, beautiful." He wasn't looking at the piano, but at his radiant wife. He traced his thumb over her rosy lips. "Play me something."

Izzy gazed at him, a faint smile forming beneath his caress. "Anything?"

"Whatever you like."

Rising gracefully from the low chaise, she wended her way between tables and chairs to the piano bench, smoothing her skirts as she sat. Her fingers danced across the keys, coaxing a series of tinkling notes, before she positioned them and began a familiar yet elusive melody.

A waltz, Sam noted, closing his eyes to savor the tune. *Where have I heard that before?*

Then his eyes popped open when she added an adorably off-key lyric in a husky voice.

Hush-a-bye, baby, on the treetop
When the wind blows, thy cradle will rock—

Sam was on his feet and kneeling at the bench before she could strike the next chord. He swept her off her seat and into his arms, both of them tangled in her skirts as they hit the floor.

He buried his lips against her fragrant throat. "A babe. My babe." He brushed a single tear from her cheek. "Are you sure?"

"As sure as possible, this early on." Winding her arms around his neck, Izzy scattered kisses everywhere she could reach. "Are you all right with this? We have been wed such a short time."

"I'm to be a father. A tiny girl who looks like her mama." Sam's heart filled so deeply and fast, it felt ready to burst.

"A small boy who could be his daddy's twin," Izzy corrected laughingly.

"One of both."

She drew back, starry-eyed. "More than one?"

Sam kissed her tenderly, lingeringly. "A houseful if you so desire, Missus Izzy," he assured her. "We'll fill our rooms with children and enjoy the making of each and every one." At her fiery cheeks, he laughed and hugged her tightly.

Against his ear she whispered, "Whatever you say, Just Sam."

Thank You from CiCi Cordelia

Dear Reader,

Thank you for joining us on this thrilling journey through the silver-rich hills of Colorado. Your support and enthusiasm for the BRIDES OF LITTLE CREEDE series mean the world to us. We hope these stories of love, courage, and new beginnings have touched your heart and transported you to a time of adventure and romance.

We invite you to continue the adventure with the complete BRIDES OF LITTLE CREEDE series. Each book offers a unique tale of love and perseverance in the Old West, but together they weave a rich tapestry of interconnected lives and shared dreams.

You can find the complete Brides of Little Creede series

on Amazon. Just search for CiCi Cordelia!

Discover More:

We'd love for you to explore more of our work and stay connected.

Here's how you can do that:

🌐 Visit our website: **CiCiWriter.com** – Where we are *Writing from the Heart*

▨ Find us on Facebook:

Thank you again for being a part of our Little Creede family. We hope you'll continue to join us for more thrilling tales of love and adventure in the Old West!

With gratitude,

Char & Cheryl, writing as CiCi Cordelia